MORE T......
MY UNCLE SILAS

Herbert Ernest Bates was born in Northamptonshire in 1905. He published his first novel, *The Two Sisters*, when he was twenty, and during the following years built up a reputation as a leading writer of great versatility. During the Second World War Bates was commissioned by the RAF as a short story writer, where he wrote the instantly acclaimed *How Sleep the Brave* and *The Greatest People in the World*. His most popular creation was the effervescent Larkin family, about whom he wrote five novels including *The Darling Buds of May* and *A Little of What You Fancy*. In 1973 H. E. Bates was awarded the CBE. He died in 1974.

H. E. Bates

MORE TALES OF
MY UNCLE SILAS

ILLUSTRATED BY
Edward Ardizzone

VINTAGE

Published by Vintage 2003

2 4 6 8 10 9 7 5 3 1

First published in Great Britain in 1957
by Michael Joseph Ltd, under the title *Sugar for the Horse*

Vintage
Random House, 20 Vauxhall Bridge Road,
London SW1V 2SA

Random House Australia (Pty) Limited
20 Alfred Street, Milsons Point, Sydney
New South Wales 2061, Australia

Random House New Zealand Limited
18 Poland Road, Glenfield,
Auckland 10, New Zealand

Random House (Pty) Limited
Endulini, 5A Jubilee Road, Parktown 2193,
South Africa

The Random House Group Limited Reg. No. 954009
www.randomhouse.co.uk

A CIP catalogue record for this book
is available from the British Library

ISBN 0 099 45356 8

Papers used by Random House are natural, recyclable
products made from wood grown in sustainable forests.
The manufacturing processes conform to the environ-
mental regulations of the country of origin

Printed and bound in Great Britain by
Bookmarque Ltd, Croydon, Surrey

Contents

Sugar for the Horse

My Uncle Silas had a little mare named Jenny, warm, brown and smooth-coated, with a cream arrow on her forehead and flecks of cream on three of her feet. She was a very knowing, friendly creature and she could take sugar off the top of your head. 'Goo anywhere and do anything,' my Uncle Silas would say. 'Only got to give her the word. Goo bed wi' me.'

'Upstairs?' I said.

'Upstairs, downstairs,' my Uncle Silas said. 'Anywhere. Where you like. I recollect——'

'Start some more tales,' my grandmother would say. 'Go on. Stuff the child's head with rubbish. Keep on. Some day he'll know the difference between the truth and what he hears from you.'

'Is the truth,' Silas said. 'She come to bed with me arter the 1897 Jubilee. Over at Kimbolton. I oughta know. There was me and Tig Flawn and Queenie White——'

'That's been a minute,' my grandmother said. She was very small and tart and dry and disbelieving. 'How old's Jenny now? Forty?'

'Well, she's gittin' on,' Silas said. 'I recollect that day Queenie had a big hat on. We got the hat off her and put it on Jenny and she come up to bed with me just like a lamb.'

'Who was Queenie White?' I said. 'Did she come to bed with you too?'

'I'm only tellin' on you about the horse,' my Uncle Silas said. 'Queenie was afore your time.'

'Pity she wasn't before yours,' my grandmother said.

'Ah, but she wadn't. Course,' he said to me, 'I could tell you a lot about her. Only you wanted to know about the horse. Well, she come to bed wi' me——'

'Did she?' my grandmother said. 'Well, I warn you here and now she'll never come to bed in no house of mine.'

Some time later my Uncle Silas came down to Nenweald Fair, on the second Sunday in August, about the time the corn was cut and the first dewberries were ripe for gathering, with Jenny in a little black trap with yellow wheels and a spray of ash-leaves on her head to keep the flies away. There was always a wonderful dinner for Nenweald Fair and Silas always kept it waiting. There was always roast beef and Yorkshire pudding and horse-radish sauce and chicken to choose from, and little kidney beans and new potatoes with butter, and yellow plum pie and cream with sugar on the pastry. There were jugs of beer on the sideboard by the clock with the picture of

Philadelphia. The batter of the Yorkshire pudding was as buttery and soft as custard and all over the house there was a wonderful smell of beef burnt at the edges by fire.

But my Uncle Silas was always late and my grandfather, an indulgent, mild-mannered man unaccustomed to revelry and things of that sort, was always full of excuses for him.

'Very like busted a belly-band coming down Longleys Hill or summat,' he would say.

'Start carving,' my grandmother would say. 'I'm having no dinner of mine spoilt for Silas or anybody else.'

'Hold hard a minute. Give him a chance.'

'The meat's on the table,' she would say, 'and if he's not here that's his lookout,' and she would plant the meat before my grandfather and it would sizzle in its gravy.

It was my Uncle Silas's custom, and my grandmother knew it and knew it only too well, not only to arrive late for that dinner but never to arrive alone. He had a habit of arriving with strange men with names like Tig Flawn and Fiddler Bollard and Slob Johnson and Tupman Jarvis. That day he arrived, about two o'clock, when most of the meat had gone and the last of the yellow plums were cooling in the dish, with a man named Ponto Pack. I always wanted him to arrive with Queenie White and see what my grandmother thought of that, but he never did and I was always rather disappointed. Whenever he did arrive my grandmother always looked as if she could hit him over the head with the pastry-board or some other suitable instrument, and that day, when I looked out of the window and saw Silas and the man Ponto, like some gigantic blond sow, falling out of the trap, I felt the carving knife would hardly have been too much.

'Let 'em all come!' my Uncle Silas roared and gave

9

prodigious beery winks from a bloodshot eye that was like a fire in a field of poppies.

'You're late,' my grandmother said. 'Get your dinner and stop shouting as if you were in Yardley Open Fields.'

'Got hung up,' Silas said. 'Belly-band broke.'

My grandmother gave my grandfather such a killing and merciless look that he went out at once to give Jenny a rub down and a drink of water, and Ponto made strange strangled noises with whole potatoes, and said, for the first of several times:

'Onaccountable. Most onaccountable.'

He was such a large man, bulging flesh as tight as bladdered lard into his suit of green-faded Sunday black, that when the rest of us had left the table it still seemed full. His eyes, pink-edged, beery, almost colourless, were uncannily like the eyes of a blond and farrowing sow. He had nothing to say all day but:

'Onaccountable, George,' or 'Onaccountable, Silas. Most onaccountable.'

In the afternoon it was very hot and everyone, including Silas, went to sleep in the front parlour or under the laurel trees, and I played giving Jenny lumps of sugar off the top of my head in the little paddock at the back of the house. I was giving her the seventh or eighth lump of sugar and wondering whether she ever did go to bed with my Uncle Silas or whether it was just another story, when my grandmother rapped on the window and said:

'Come you in out of that sun. You'll never stay awake tonight without you get some rest.'

She must have known what was coming. About half-past six my Uncle Silas and my grandfather and Ponto Pack had another jug of beer in the shade of the laurel trees and my Uncle Silas, wet-lipped, bloodshot eye

wickedly cocked, began to talk about 'gittin' the belly-band mended while we think on it.' It did not seem to me to be a thing that wanted thinking on at all, and I do not think my grandmother thought so either. She had put on her grey silk dress with the parma violet stitching at the collar and her little high hat with michaelmas daisies on the brim, and it was time now to be thinking of 'walking up street.' To walk up street on the Sunday of Nenweald Fair was a gentle, ponderous, respectable, long-winded custom, and it was something about which neither my Uncle Silas, my grandfather nor Ponto Pack seemed, I thought, very enthusiastic.

'You goo steady on up,' Silas said. 'We'll come on arter we git the belly-band mended.'

'If everything was as right as that belly-band nobody would hurt much,' she said.

'It's too 'nation hot yit for traipsing about,' Silas said.

'Onaccountable hot,' Ponto said. 'Most onaccountable.'

Ten minutes later the trap went jigging past us up the street, my Uncle Silas wearing his black-and-white deer-stalker sideways on, so that the peaks stuck out like ears, and Ponto, bowler hat perched on the top of his head like a cannon ball, looking more than ever like some pink-eyed performing pig. My grandfather pretended not to see us and my grandmother said:

'What one doesn't think of, the other will. The great fool things.'

We seemed to take longer than ever that sultry evening to make the tour under the chestnut trees about the crowded market-place. I always got very bored with the gossiping Sunday-starched crowd of bowler hats and parasols and I kept thinking how nice it would be if my Uncle Silas were to come back with Jenny and I could do my trick of giving her sugar, in full view of everybody, off the top of my head. But Silas never came and by ten o'clock I was yawning and my grandmother had even stopped saying darkly, whenever there was something nice to listen to, 'Little pigs have got big ears,' as if I hadn't the vaguest idea of what she meant by that.

I went to bed with a piece of cold Yorkshire pudding to eat and fell asleep with it in my hands. It is hard to say now what time I woke up, but what woke me was like the thunder of one crazy dream colliding with another some-where at the foot of the stairs. The piece of cold Yorkshire pudding was like a frog crawling on my pillow, and I remember wanting to shriek about it just at the moment I heard my Uncle Silas roaring in the front passage:

'Git up, old gal! Git up there! Pull up, old gal!'

A terrifying sound as of madly-beaten carpets greeted me at the top of the stairs. It was my grandmother beating Ponto Pack across the backside with what I thought was the stick we used for stirring pig-swill. She could not get at my Uncle Silas because Silas was leading Jenny up the stairs; and she could not get at my grandfather because he was lying like a sack of oats on Jenny's back. Ponto was pushing Jenny with his round black backside sticking out like a tight balloon and my Uncle Silas kept bawling:

'Git underneath on her, Ponto. You ain't underneath on her.'

Every time Ponto seemed about to git underneath on her my grandmother hit him again with the swill-stick. I thought he did not seem to mind very much. He laughed every time my grandmother hit him and then pushed himself harder than ever against Jenny's hindquarters and called with pig-like fruitiness to my Uncle Silas, tugging at the bridle on the stairs:

'Can't budge the old gal, Silas. Most aggravatin' onaccountable.'

'Get that mare out of my house, you drunken idiots!' my grandmother shrieked.

'Gotta git George to bed fust,' Silas said. 'Must git George to bed.'

'Get that horse off my stair-carpet!'

'Gotta git George to bed. Good gal!' Silas said. 'Come on now, good gal. Tchck, tchck! Up, mare! That's a good gal.'

By this time my Uncle Silas had succeeded in tugging Jenny a quarter of the way upstairs when suddenly, down below, sharp and sickening above the pandemonium of voices, there was a crack like a breaking bone. Ponto Pack roared, 'Silas, she's hittin' me on the coconut!' and at the same moment Jenny had something like hysterics, whinnying terribly, and fell down on her front knees on the stairs. My Uncle Silas yelled, 'Why th' Hanover don't you git underneath on her? She'll be down atop on y'!' and for a moment I thought she was. She gave a great lurch backwards and my grandfather let out a groan. My grandmother hit Ponto another crack on the head with the swill-stick and suddenly the whole essence of the situation became, to me at any rate, splendidly clear. My Uncle Silas and Ponto were trying to get my grandfather to bed and my grandmother, in her obstinate way, was trying to stop them.

I remembered in that moment the cold Yorkshire pudding. I fetched it from my bedroom and went half-way down the stairs and held it out to Jenny, most coaxingly, in the flat of my hand.

Whether she thought, at that moment, that I in my white nightshirt was some kind of newly-woken ghost or whether she decided she had had enough of the whole affair, I never knew. Ponto had hardly time to bawl out from the bottom of the stairs, 'It's most onaccountable, Silas. I can't budge her!' and my Uncle Silas from the top of the stairs, 'Hold hard, Pont. The old gal's knockin' off for a mite o' pudden!' when my grandmother, aiming another crack at Ponto's head, hit the mare in her fury a blow above the tail.

The frenzy of her hysterical ascent up three steps of stairs and then backwards down the whole flight was something I shall not forget. My grandfather fell off the mare and the mare fell sideways on him, and then my Uncle Silas fell on the mare. The three of them fell on

my grandmother and my grandmother fell on Ponto Pack.
My Uncle Silas yelled, 'Let 'em all come!' and my
grandmother hit Ponto twenty or thirty blows on the top
of the head with the swill-stick. My grandfather fell off
the horse's back and landed with a terrible crash on the
umbrella-stand, and the portrait of Gladstone fell down
in the hall. The cold Yorkshire pudding fell down the
stairs and I fell after it. My aunt came in the front door
with a policeman, and Ponto yelled, 'It's onaccountable,
Silas, most onaccountable!' just as the mare broke free
and charged the sideboard in the front room.

My Uncle Silas sat on the bottom of the stairs and
laughed his head off, and I began to cry because I was
sorry for Jenny and thought it was the end of the world.

The Bedfordshire Clanger

MY Uncle Silas was very fixed and very firm in the notion
that women were no good to you. 'They're allus arter
you, boy,' he said. 'Allus arter you.'

I was, at the time, very small, and it was much too soon
for me to point out that Silas, on the contrary, was
always arter them.

'Like her,' he said. 'Take her. Allus arter me.'

At the age of ninety-one my Uncle Silas still had
something of the look of a crusty farmyard cock. He gave
a great sniffing sort of sigh, fixed his bloodshot eye on me
in cunning reminiscence and whipped a dewdrop off his
nose.

'She wadn' half a tartar,' he said. 'Everlastin' arter me.
Night and day.'

'Doing what?' I said.

'Plaguing on me.'

'For what?'

'Tormentin' on me,' he said. 'Whittlin' me to death.'

His bloodshot eye had a crack of scarlet glee across it.

'What was her name?' I said.

'Tutts,' he said.

'That's a funny name.'

'She wur a funny woman,' he said. 'She wur very near the death on me.'

Since my Uncle Silas had reached the nineties and looked, in his leathery and ruddy heartiness, good for another dozen years, it seemed a very good moment to ask how death by Miss Tutts had been avoided so long ago.

'I give her gee-up,' he said. 'That's how.'

It seemed a very good moment also to ask how he had given her gee-up, and if possible why and what with, but he surprised me a little when the answer came.

'I laid her out with a Bedfordshire clanger,' he said.

I did not know what a Bedfordshire clanger was, and it occurred to me for a moment that it was an awful sort of lie. But he said:

'Sort o' pudden. Suet. Hard as a hog's back.'

We were sitting among the gooseberry bushes at the time, by the bottom of Silas's garden, under the wood, where sun lay warm by a fringe of hazels. Gooseberries, ripe and golden-green and fat as plums, bowed down the branches of the squat trees, and now and then Silas lazily pinched one with crabbed fingers and split it open and shot its sweet jellied seeds on to his ripe and ruby tongue.

'Kept a boarding-house,' he said.

For some moments he squirted gooseberry seeds into his mouth and chewed through what I hoped were moments of reminiscence, champing at the sourer skin. His gills seemed to laugh up and down, from the acid of the gooseberries, like the gills of an old and crusty cock.

'Them are the ones you want to be careful on,' he said.

I bit on a gooseberry too. Silas fixed his eyes on a point somewhere far away and I could smell the strong odour of corduroys warm in the sun.

'Young chap at the time,' he said. 'That's all. Apprentice. Innocent young chap.'

It has always been difficult for me to conjure up a picture of my Uncle Silas at the age of innocence, but I did not say anything and he went on:

'Me an' Arth Sugars' he said. 'We boarded together.'

I wanted to know who Arth Sugars was and he said:

'Arth wadn't all ninepence. Had a kink somewhere. Wanted to be inventor.'

'What did he invent?'

'Well, for a start-off nothing much,' he said. 'But then I got there——'

He picked another gooseberry and squashed it against his tongue and gave a great sucking sound at the bursting purse of seeds. 'Chronic,' he said several times. 'Chronic,' and then went on suddenly with a horrible reminiscence of that far-off boarding-house, where he and Mr. Sugars, the inventor, had starved.

'Day in and day out,' he said, 'the same sort o' grub. No different. Week-days and Sundays. No different. Allus the same.'

'What grub?'

'Pudden. Just pudden.'

'What sort?'

'Plain.'

He shook his head with great sadness so that I, too, could feel how terrible it was.

'Think on it,' he said. 'Dinner—tea—supper, week in, week out, months on it. Just plain.'

'Suet?'

He turned on me with a horrible sort of bark that made me feel ashamed. 'It might have been suet *once*,' he said. 'But when we got it—ah! boy, it wur harder 'n prison bread.'

He paused and at that moment I suddenly discovered a defect in all this. I could not picture Miss Tutts. I could not conceive what sort of person, physically, she was.

'I wur coming to that,' he said. 'Whady' *think* she was?'

'Think?'

'Ah,' he said. 'Fat or thin?'

'Thin,' I said.

He cried out with a bark of triumph.

'I knowed you'd say that. Thin, you says, eh? You think she wur thin, you says. She wur mean and a tartar, so she must be thin? Eh? Ain't that it?'

'I suppose I——'

'Well, you're supposing wrong. Fat—that's what she wur. Like a twenty-score sow in pig.'

He looked at me with such an air of pained and sharp correction that I said I was sorry I had been mistaken.

'And a good thing for you. 'Cause now you'll *understand* better, see? Her so fat and me an' Arth so thin. It makes it wuss, don't it? Makes it chronic, don't it, eh?'

I said it made it very chronic. I said something, too, about how greatly they must have suffered, and he said:

'Suffered? We suffered till we couldn't suffer no longer.'

19

'And then what did you do?'

'Put paid to her,' he said.

I asked him how they put paid to her. Slowly he squeezed another gooseberry against his bright red tongue and said:

'Fust of all we give her a Seidlitz powder.'

'Wasn't she very well?' I said.

'Oh! she wur well,' he said, 'but we jis' wanted to see what happened. We jis' put the Seidlitz powder in the ——, well, that don't matter now. Have another gooseberry, boy. Help yourself to another gooseberry.'

I helped myself to another gooseberry and said I hated Seidlitz powders.

'They fizz,' I said.

'Thass it,' he said. 'Thass just it. They fizz.'

His gills began laughing again with the droll shagginess of an old cock and I said:

'Didn't it make a difference?'

'Well, it made a difference,' he said, 'in a way. But not to us.'

'The puddings didn't get better?'

'Not until arterwards,' he said darkly. 'Not until arterwards.'

My Uncle Silas relapsed into a veiled and secret sort of meditation, one eye closed. He did not speak for some time and I began to grow impatient to know what lay behind that arterwards. I was afraid for some moments that he would fall asleep there, in the warm July air among the gooseberry bushes, and never tell me.

Presently I nudged him and asked him not to go to sleep and he flickered an eye:

'Don't whittle me, boy,' he said. 'I'm a-recollectin' on it.'

He suddenly gave an immense and fruity chuckle, something like a joyful belch partly arrested. It was the sound I knew, long afterwards, as something always preceding the greatest lie. Then he shook his head as if it were all terribly serious and said:

'Millions on 'em.'

'Millions of what?' I said.

'Puddens.'

He did not look at me. He fixed his bloodshot, wicked eye on the distance and grunted, 'Never see nothing like it, boy, you never see nothing like it,' and then went on to tell me, between winey belches that rippled out of his corduroyed belly like waves, how he and Arth Sugars, tired of that long prison diet of suet, decided to discover for themselves how Miss Tutts made and kept up the supply; and how they crept down to the basement at midnight, with a candle, and found there, in rows upon rows, on high shelves, enough puddings to feed an army.

'Millions on 'em,' he said. 'All wrapped up in old ham-bags and shimmies and skirts an'——'

'What did you do?' I said.

'Filled 'em.'

I asked him how they filled them and what with, and he said, airily:

'Different flavours.'

'Strawberry and raspberry?'

'Ah! better'n that,' he said. 'Some on 'em we filled with brimstone. Then we had a Seidlitz or two. A few Epsoms. Then some as Arth invented. Then I don't know as we didn't have a ——, well, anyway, we wur half-way through the brimstone when we had company.'

'Who?'

'Her,' he said.

He shook his head.

'Never see nothing like it in your life. Half-starve naked. In her nightshirt.'

'Enough to catch her death,' I said.

'It wur,' he said. 'There wur we a-top of a step-ladder, and there wur Arth holdin' the candle and a-givin' me the different flavours. I wur just pickin' a pudden up when she come ravin' in——'

'What happened?' I said.

'Dropped it,' he said.

'On her?'

'On her,' he said. 'Give her such a clout—it jis' shows you how hard they was, jis' shows you—give her such a clout she wur cold in a couple o' seconds.'

'That was awful,' I said. 'What did you do?'

'Awful,' he said. 'Do? Arth run upstairs like a hare for a burnt feather and the smellin' salts.'

'Yes,' I said, 'but what did you do?'

'Kept her warm,' he said. 'Thass what you got to do when folks are cold, ain't it? And she wur very cold, I tell you boy, in that there nightgown. Very cold.'

I did not speak. A little doubt assailed me. I could not in that moment reconcile the picture of my Uncle Silas keeping Miss Tutts warm in the basement at midnight with the way the story had begun. There seemed, suddenly, great discrepancies somewhere. Hadn't it begun by Miss Tutts tormenting him? Hadn't she been a terror, a plague, and a tartar? It seemed very strange to me that plaguing and tormenting and pursuit could end with Miss Tutts being warmed in my Uncle Silas's arms. Strange that things could change so quickly.

'And did things change?' I said. 'You know—the puddens. Were they better?'

My Uncle Silas fixed his roving bloodshot eye on the distance and with a delicious spurting juicy sound, squirted the seeds of another gooseberry against his tongue.

'Arter that,' he said, 'I wur never in want fur the nicest bit o' pudden in the world.'

Queenie White

THE name of Queenie White was hardly ever mentioned in our family, except of course by my Uncle Silas, who was inclined to mention it rather frequently.

'Now that wur the year when me and Queenie——'

'We don't want to hear it, thank you, we don't want to hear it, we don't want to hear it!'

'Now wait half a jiff,' Silas would say. 'If you can hold your horses I wur going to say as that wur the year we had snow in July——'

'We know all about it, thank you. We know all about it. We know *all* about it.'

The trouble was that everyone else except myself seemed to know all about it and it was on an afternoon in

September, many years later, before I was able to clear up the mystery of the unmentionable Queenie White and what she had done, if anything, to make her name resound so unspeakably in the ears of the women of my family.

That afternoon I walked over to see my Uncle Silas, taking with me a drop of something I thought would please his palate, and as we sat in the garden, in the drowsy wasp-laden air, under a big tree of Blenheim apples, he turned to me and said:

'This is a drop o' good, boy. Red-currant, ain't it?'

I said that it was red-currant and he rolled another mouthful of it over his thick red tongue before saying:

'It's a bit sharper 'n elderberry and it ain't so flowery as cowslip, but it's proper more-ish all the same. Proper more-ish.'

A moment later he started to look very dreamy, as he always did in the act of recollecting something far away, and said:

'You know the last time I tasted red-currant? It's bin about forty years agoo—over at *The Cat and Custard Pot*, at Swineshead.' He gave one of those ripe, solemn pauses of his. 'Wi' Queenie White.'

It was always a good thing not to hurry my Uncle Silas in the matter of these more distant recollections and I did not say a word. I poured him another glass of red-currant wine instead and after some moments he picked up the glass and gazed softly through the pure bright wine, an even purer and sharper crimson than the half-transparent, polished currants themselves had been, and said:

'Yis: she kept *The Cat and Custard Pot*, or any road she and her husband did.'

I said I was surprised to hear that Queenie White was married but he said blandly:

'Oh! yis. Married all right. Well, that is if you could call Charley White a man. He wur more like a damn bean pole with a boiled egg stuck on top.'

I must confess that I was not as interested in the appearance of Charley White as in what a woman called Queenie could possibly look like, but there was no hurrying my Uncle Silas, who shook his head in slow disgust and suddenly let out one of those rare-flavoured rural words of his.

'Maungy,' he said. 'That's what he wur, Charley White. Maungy. A mean, maungy, jealous man.'

I don't suppose you are ever likely to find the word maungy in any dictionary but the effect it gives is, I think, a very expressive one. You get the impression of something between mingy and mangy and I knew at once, in this case, that Charley White could only have been a mean, moody misery of a man.

'Wuss 'n a chapel deacon,' my Uncle Silas said. 'Allus countin' the ha'pence and puttin' a padlock on the fardens. If it hadn't been for Queenie the pub'd never ha' sold a ha'poth o' homebrewed to a stray tom-cat in a month o' Sundays.'

By this time I was more eager than ever to hear what Queenie White had looked like, but my Uncle Silas said:

'Yis, an' a lot older 'n her too. Perhaps he'd told her the tale pretty well and she thought he'd got money but I be damned if I know how she ever got married to that streak o' horse ——. Well, never mind, she wur, poor gal, and she had to put up wi' it.'

Then: 'Or any road she did till she met me.'

In the very expressive pause that followed I had a moment of recollection myself and said:

' "Jalous he was and held her narwe in cage; for she was wild and young and he was old." '

'What wur that you jist said?' my Uncle Silas asked sharply.

'That was a line of poetry,' I said, 'about a carpenter and his wife. By a man named Chaucer. It made me think of Queenie White.'

'Chaucer?' he said. 'Any kin to old Blunderbuss Chaucer over at Stanwick Woods? He wur a rate old poachin' man.'

'No,' I said, 'this Chaucer was a long way before your time.'

'Then he must have been a fly 'un,' my Uncle Silas said.

After that he took another drink of red-currant wine, afterwards brushing the back of his hand across his wet red lips, and then went on to tell me how, in her narrow cage, where even the farthings were padlocked, Queenie White did all the work, attracted all the customers and never had a night's fun or day's outing from one year's end to another.

'Very sad gal, Queenie,' he said. 'Proper un'appy.'

'You might tell me what she looked like,' I said.

'Queenie? Big,' he said. 'A very big gal.'

He licked his lips slowly.

'And when I say big I don't mean ugly big.' He lowered his voice a fraction. 'I mean beautiful big.'

The wine, I thought, was beginning to inspire him now and he went on:

'You've 'eerd talk o' gals with them titty little waists what you can get your two hands round? Well, Queenie'd got a waist like a big sheaf o' corn—summat big and strong you could git holt on. Solid. And legs an' arms like a mare. And upstairs——'

27

Here he glanced, I thought, at the upstairs windows of the house, as if thinking that someone might be looking down on us from there, but instead he was really preparing, as I heard a moment later, to complete the description of Queenie White.

'Beautiful bosom,' he said. 'Like a winder ledge. You could a' laid a bunch o' flowers on it easy as pie.'

This charming picture of the upper parts of Queenie White's figure brought her fully to my mind's eye at last, except for one thing.

'What colour hair?' I asked him.

He seemed for a moment uncertain, I thought, about the colour of Queenie White's hair, and he paused for several moments longer, pondering on it.

'If I wur to tell you it wur just about the colour of the sand that day we nipped off to the sea,' he said at last, 'that'd be about as near as I could git to it.'

'The sea?'

'Yis,' he said, 'the sea. We done a bunk together.'

He ruminated a little more on this, stooping down after some moments to pick up a big fallen apple from the grass. After he had polished this apple on his corduroy trousers he held it up to me, clenching it hard in his hands.

'She wur as firm as that there apple,' he said. 'Beautiful an' firm. No: she wadn't one o' them Skinny Lizzies, Queenie, all gristle and bone and suet. They didn't call her Queenie for nothing—and I tell you, boy, that's what she looked like. A red-'eaded queen.'

All this, I thought, was so interesting that I poured him another glass of red-currant wine. And again, before drinking, he held it up to the light of the clear September afternoon. All the ripeness of late summer floated down through it, pouring on to his crusty hands a tender crimson glow.

'What I can't a-bear is a man what's maungy,' he said. 'A man what's jealous. I see that gal a-working night an' day there and him a-locking the fardens up and skin-flintin' over every pint o' beer and a-fiddle-faddlin' over how many matches in a box. God A'mighty I believe he grudged breathin' too often—he hated wastin' 'is breath. He even grudged her peelin' the skin too thick off a tater. Yis!—God's truth, I be dalled if he didn't measure a tater skin one day. Told her it wur too thick to give to pigs!'

You didn't often see my Uncle Silas in a state of anger, but suddenly he lifted the apple and threw it violently across the garden, where it burst on the pig-sty door.

'That's what I'd a-like to ha' done to 'im,' he said. 'Throwed 'im up against the 'ug-sty. Instead o' that I said to myself "Silas," I said, "you're a-goin' to give that there young gal one day in her life as she'll never forgit if she lives till bull's-noon." '

It was June, he said, when they did their bunk together. They waited until the long, bald, jealous bean-pole of a husband had gone off to market one Wednesday—'allus went skin-flintin' off to market of a Wednesday wi' a couple of rabbits or a hare or a brace o' birds some old poacher had brought in to swop fer a pint—allus on the mek-haste, never 'ettin' on 'em, no blamed fear, not Charley'—and Silas could drive her to the station in a trap.

That day she was wearing a big white hat with an ostrich feather that she hadn't worn since the day she was married and a mauve-coloured coat with big black buttons and silk frogs across the front. I imagined her to look splendidly gay and fresh and excited: exactly, as Silas said, like a queen.

The bunk, he was careful to explain several times, was only for the day.

'I wanted her to 'ave jist one damn good day she'd allus remember,' he said. 'Hang about Charley. Hang about the old tits a-gossipin'. Hang about whether she wur a married woman. Hang about the consequences. Dammit! What the 'Anover are we 'ere for? Not to be maungy old narrer-gutses like Charley White, I tell you! We're dead a long time.'

If there had been another apple at hand at this moment he would, I believe, have hurled that too at the pig-sty door.

'Sea wur beautiful,' he said. 'She'd never seen the sea afore. Couldn't credit it. Beautiful blue. Beautiful an' calm. Beautiful sand. She couldn't credit it. We lay there aside of a big sand-dune very nearly all day a-starin' at it. And then——'

He broke off and in the long expectant pause that followed I saw that his glass was almost empty. I started to fill it up again and then noticed that, for once, he was hardly watching me. His eyes were resting softly on the September distances, as if he were actually staring at the sea.

'Then what?' I said.

'Then she done summat terrible onexpected,' he said.

He drank, wiping his mouth. I waited, and again he shook his head.

'Wouldn't go home,' he said.

He stared thoughtfully into his glass, putting it slowly down.

'Couldn't turn her,' he said. 'Wouldn't budge. Couldn't git round her nohow.'

I at once pointed out that he had, after all, got round her easily enough to do the bunk in the first place, and he readily agreed that this was so.

'Yis, but that wur when she wur *low*,' he said. 'It's easy to git round wimmin when they're low. But arter a day at the sea wi' me she wur a different woman.'

I said that I did not doubt at all that any woman would be.

'Arter all,' he said, 'if you turn a nag out into a medder where the grass is sweet it ain't likely he's a-goin' back all that eager to eat chaff and wezzles in a stable, is it?'

I agreed. 'But what did you do?'

'Had to give in to the gal,' he said. 'Dall it, it wur awk'ard, though.'

It had never been a particularly remarkable feature of my Uncle Silas's character, I thought, to find such situations awkward, but in this case he was very quick to enlighten me.

'For one thing I hadn't got the money,' he said. 'I'd on'y come out fer the day.'

'I'm sure that worried you,' I said. 'How much longer did you stay?'

'Best part of a fortnit.'

'On whose money?'

'Her'n,' he said. 'Or rather it wur Charley's. She'd been fly enough to bring it with her.'

It now began to be borne upon me why the name of Queenie White had been, for so many years, an unspeakable one in our family.

'It wur oncommon awk'ard,' my Uncle Silas said. 'But arter a few days I started to git used to it.'

Remembering Queenie White's waist that was like a sheaf of corn, her limbs that were like a mare's and her splendid bosom on which you might have laid a bunch of flowers, I did not think that getting used to it could, after all, have been so very difficult.

'Then the money run out.'

'Made quite a difference, I suppose?'

He pondered.

'Well, it did in a way,' he said, 'but not half so much difference as Charley White did when he turned up.'

He took a rapid drink, as if fortifying himself, and I filled up his glass again.

'I wisht you could ha' seen that there fight, boy,' he said. 'It wur a proper stack-up. Me a little 'un and him that long thin streak o' goat's —— boy, it wur a proper rare 'un, that wur.'

I filled up my own glass this time and urged him on with murmurs of approbation.

'Fust he hit me with a pint pot,' my Uncle Silas said. 'Well, I'd be damned if I wur a-standin' that, so I hit him wi' one. Then he fetched me a couple o' rip-tearing snorters across the chops and I hit him one in the bread basket. Then he blacked my eye and I blacked one of his'n back again. Arter that I dunno what he did hit me with. It felt like a damn cannon ball or summat and I started sailing down the Milky Way. When I come round——'

The admission that my Uncle Silas had been laid out quite startled me, but not nearly so much as the fact that he suddenly started roaring with laughter.

'You never see anything so damn' funny in your life, boy.'

He took a deep swig of wine and slapped his other hand down on his knee.

'What was going on?' I said.

'Queenie wur givin' *'im* a good hidin',' he said. 'Ah! an' it wur a good 'un too. I told you how big an' strong she was. Well, she wur a-mowin' into 'im like a Irishman a-mowin' into a forty-acre field o' barley.'

'Pleasant sight,' I said.

'Not fer 'im it wadn't,' he said. 'When she'd finished with 'im he looked as if he'd been through a mangle back'ards. He wur a-layin' flat on 'is back sayin' "No, Queenie, no, please, that's enough o' that!" and she wur a-wipin' the floor with 'im. And then when it wur all over she picked 'im up and dragged 'im off like a rabbit skin.'

'Home?'

'Home,' he said.

'And did you,' I said, 'go on seeing her after that?'

'Course they wur a big scandal,' he said. 'You bet your breeches they wur. All the old tits wur a-twitterin' an' a-gossipin' an' a-maunderin' about it fer years. Couldn't stop talkin' about it. Loved it. Couldn't forgit it. Just their drop.'

'But did you——'

'Oh! yes, I used to see her,' he said. 'Used to see her quite often. She got out a good deal arter that, happy as you like, when she liked and how she liked. Oh! yis, she wur a free woman arter that. She wur boss arter that.'

Pondering on the word free, I found it difficult to phrase what was in my mind. Running away with another man's wife was, it seemed to me, not altogether a light affair and what I wanted to know was if my Uncle Silas perhaps——

'I know what you're a-thinkin',' he said. 'You're a-wonderin' if me an' Queenie—well, we never. She wur a good gal arter that. The only thing was——'

'Yes?' I said.

'I used to take her a bunch o' flowers sometimes of a Sunday,' he said.

He slowly lifted his glass, staring through it, and I saw once again how the red glow of it poured on to his crusty hand a tender pool of light. About us, under the tree, the air was full of the hum of wasps as they worked among the fallen September apples and for some moments longer his voice was hardly louder than the sound of wings as he described for me how Queenie White would hold the flowers to her face, rest them on her splendid bosom and talk briefly of the beauty of the sea.

Suddenly he clasped my own hand in his own oyster-crusty palm.

'Mek the most on it while you can, boy,' he said. 'Take a tip from Silas—mek the most on it while you can.'

He stared with dreamy contemplation at the last of his wine.

'Course she's dead now,' he said. 'Bin dead a good while. But I often wonder whether I shall see her—you know, up there. That's if I ever goo.'

'You'll go,' I said.

'I ain't so sure,' he said. 'But I know one thing—there ain't a better-lookin' gal up there.'

With that certain air of sadness that sometimes overlaid his devilry he once more contemplated the soft September distances, raised his glass and then blessed the name of the woman whose waist was like a sheaf of corn and on whose queenly bosom you could have laid a bunch of flowers.

'Mek the most on it while you can, boy,' he said. 'Mek the most on it while you can.'

The Blue Feather

I ONCE made a chance remark to my Uncle Silas that had the remarkable effect of making him turn quite pale.

'I was going by Castle Hanwick yesterday,' I started to say.

'God A'mighty boy, don't mention that there place to me,' he said. 'God A'mighty.'

Ordinarily my Uncle Silas's face presented a plummy mixture of reds and purples, with the bright veins of his bloodshot eye most fierily pronounced; but now a distinct pallor, I thought, began to spread through what he always called his gills.

'Don't mention that there place,' he said again. 'It fair curdles me. I had a terrible narrer squeak there.'

I thought I detected in this the beginnings of some ill-timed amorous adventure, such as my Uncle Silas being locked in a still room with a parlour-maid or having perhaps to cope with the unexpected misfortune of being found under, if not in, the mistress's bed; but I was mistaken.

'Poachin',' he said. 'Well, I'd *bin* a-poachin', we'll say that. No denyin' that. Got a couple o' brace of pheasants on fish-hooks and raisins—nothing much. That never worrited me. It wur what 'appened arterwards what prit' near cooked me.'

His gills, I noticed, had by this time recovered their customary ruby health, though his voice still quavered.

'I tell you, boy,' he said, 'I wur prit' near cooked that time.'

He then began to describe for my benefit, as if I had never seen it before, the house at Castle Hanwick and its surroundings. It is one of those great mansions, not castle-like in shape, though a castle in name, that stand splendidly on the escarpment of the middle, flowery reaches of the River Ouse, overlooking the river twisting on its many turns across the reedy meadows below. The place has been sold up now and they keep idiots there, or prisoners without bars: it hardly matters which. But in my day, and still more in my Uncle Silas's day, the land bloomed and yielded in splendidly ordered pattern and fertility above the valley, its woodlands full of game and foxes, its park carrying a herd of deer which you could see sometimes flicking away in fear beyond big roundels of copper-beeches.

These, at any rate, were my own impressions, but my Uncle Silas said, when I mentioned the Castle's late lost lushness:

'Ah! I know: it wur like that one time and it wur like that agin. But round about '85 it wur a sight different. It changed a terrible lot about that time.'

He broke off and was silent and I thought for a moment, as he actually closed his eyes, that he was going to drop off into one of those cock-like uncommunicative dozes of his, when he would suddenly wake up and say: 'Lost meself for a moment, boy. Where wur I?'

This time I gave him no chance. 'You were saying you were poaching.'

'So I wur,' he said. 'One October morning. Bin at it all night and jist nippin' back home. Got the pheasants in a sack with about half a hundredweight o' water-creeses a-top on 'em.'

He went on to say how beautiful the water-cresses had been in a little brook that ran down through the southern end of the parkland. 'Very frem,' he said, using one of those good local words of his. 'Frem and young. Bin a very good late season for 'em that year.'

I now reminded him of his remark about how much the place had changed round about 1885 and he said:

'That's right. Gone to rack and ruin. The old man of all, old St. John Featherstone, died about 1882. Terrible gambler—spent most of his time in clubs in London. And in two or three years you couldn't see the place for briars and nettles. Like a damn jungle everywhere.'

'But still pheasants.'

'Oh yis, pheasants,' he said. 'I ain't sayin' they wadn't no pheasants. Else I shouldn't ha' bin there. What I'm a-sayin' is that a few year afore that your life wouldn't ha' bin worth 'atful o' crabs if you'd ha' bin seen even starin' over the fence. Keepers everywhere. Armies on 'em. On sentry.'

That October morning my Uncle Silas skirted a bed of osiers by the brook and worked his way southward across the park, taking advantage of the coverts, just as day was breaking. He was feeling pretty cocksure, safe and pleased with himself when, as he hopped over a stile at the end of an avenue of big straggling rhododendrons, a man popped up out of the bushes and barred his way with a six-foot ash-pole.

'I wur never more surprised in me life,' Silas said. 'It fair took the wind out on me.'

'Keeper?'

'Oh! no,' he said. 'Oh! no. No sich thing. It was 'im 'isself. Eldest son. The young St. John Featherstone. Well: I say young. Man about sixty I should say.

'Difficult situation.'

'Oh! no,' he said. 'Oh! no. Never bothered me a bit. Wouldn't ha' bothered you either if you'd ha' seen im.'

'What was he like?'

'Well,' he said, 'I'll tell you. Give you a rough idea on 'im if I can. Tall man, terrible thin and bent over at the top, like a parson a-prayin'. Very holler-chested, with a gruet big Adam's apple like a pump handle stickin' out over one o' them high starched collars. Straw hat on his head—October, mind you—and big fishin' boots over 'is cricket flannels. What d'ye make o' that?'

It was really not necessary, as I well knew, to say what I made of it.

'And the face?' I said.

'Looked like a blood'ound out o' sorts,' my Uncle Silas said.

Here my Uncle Silas raised his voice and started to give an imitation of the accents of the English aristocracy.

' "My man," he says, he says, "what you a-got in that there bag, my man, eh?" So I says water-creeses, sir, I said, water-creeses, sir, on'y water-creeses, and then he cackled like a gander and said, "Ho, so it's only water-creeses is it, it's only water-creeses? In that there case," he says, "in that there case," he says, "my man, I suppose they have feathers on?" And I looked down and I be damned if they wasn't a pheasant feather stickin' out of a hole in the sack.'

'You were cooked,' I said.

My Uncle Silas, ignoring this, went on with his imitation of the English aristocracy.

' "My man," he says, he says, "my man, you've a-bin a-poachin'. I know, I know," he says, "you've a-bin a-poachin'. And in that there case, my man," he says, "in that there case, you'll have the goodness to come up to the house with me." '

I remarked for a second time how my Uncle Silas seemed to be cooked, but again he ignored me and went on to tell how there had been nothing for it but to go up to the house, quietly.

'Not that I were worrit,' he said. 'We'd got a bridge to go over and I got it worked out I could drop the bag in the river when he wadn't lookin'. But it never come orf— he kept me in front on 'im all the time.'

'Now you were cooked,' I said.

He turned on me quite sharply.

'Dammit, don't keep a-sayin' I wur cooked,' he said. 'That's later. You allus want to git on sich a 'nation long way ahead. It took days, this 'ere affair. It took weeks. I wadn't cooked till later—and then'—here he cocked his head at me with severe remonstration—'on'y damn near see? on'y *damn near*.'

I had sometimes known him to break off a tale in the middle and never resume it. And remembering it, I was quiet after that, trying not to upset him, simply listening.

'I jist recollected one more thing as 'appened when we went up to the 'ouse,' he said. 'Funny thing—I don't know what made me do it, but I spotted a jay's feather that had dropped on a blackberry bush and I picked it up as we went by and put it in me cap. Stuck it in a-one side.'

The incident did not seem of very great importance to me and I was careful to say nothing about it.

'Any road,' he said, 'we got to the house and the old bird locked me up in a room. I wur there about a hour and I thought he'd gone for old Bill Bollard, the policeman. Course I knowed Bill well. We wur 'and-in-glove most o' the time.'

Soon after the hour was up there was a rattling of a key in the lock and the door opened and in came, to my Uncle Silas's considerable surprise, the cook.

'Gal named Em Pack,' he said. 'She hadn't been there very long. Very particular sort o' gal. Bit miserable. Chapel.'

And what she had to say also surprised my Uncle Silas considerably.

'Your breakfast is ready,' she said. 'You'd better come and eat it while you can.'

He followed her into the kitchen, where she put before him a plate of bacon and two eggs. 'You can have three if you like,' she said. 'Or four, or five, or half-a-dozen. I don't care. I'm leaving tomorrow anyway.'

My Uncle Silas said he did not at all mind the prospect

of a third egg or a couple of extra rashers of bacon and presently she cooked these too and put them before him.

'Then,' my Uncle Silas said, 'she started 'orse-facin' at me. An' if there's anything I can't a-bear it is being 'orse-faced at by wimmin. Said I ought to know better, poachin' an' trespassin' on other people's property. Said I ought to be ashamed o' meself. Said it would serve me right when I went *up there*.

'I didn't know what she meant by *up there* at the time,' my Uncle Silas said, 'so I asked her why she wur leaving.'

'Never you mind,' she said. 'You'll see.'

'See what?' he asked her.

'You'll see,' she said. 'When you get *up there*. When *she* gets hold of you.'

If there was any prospect from which my Uncle Silas did not shrink it was that of being got hold of by a woman and he ate his eggs and bacon calmly to the end. They were very good indeed, he said, and the only thing lacking was a glass of beer to wash them down.

'You'll get no beer here,' she snapped, 'so I'll tell you. And I'll tell you something else—you want to be sober when you go up there or else I'll be blamed if you won't think you're seeing things.'

'Well, I ain't seed things on a pint yit,' he said, 'but I dessay there's always a fust time.'

After that he finished his bacon and eggs and presently he was going upstairs, cap in hand, with the young St. John Featherstone, the ailing, drooping bloodhound. The house, as he described it, was dark and gloomy. Ancestral portraits, flanked by numbers of swords, battle-axes and breast-plates, hung on the walls about the stairs. A few moulting fox-heads, keeping funereal company with a

stag's head or two and a scraggy badger, filled the peeling walls of the landings beyond.

'My sister will see you now,' the drooping bloodhound said. 'It is her place to deal with you.'

A moment or two later the old bloodhound knocked on a door, opened it and ushered my Uncle Silas into a room.

'And there she wur,' he said. 'This 'ere female.'

The word female is, at this point, a most important one. My Uncle Silas referred to the opposite sex, generally, in four main categories: gals, old gals, wimmin and females. He might occasionally refer also to ladies, young fillies, old tits and possibly bits of fancy goods. I have heard him also speak of wenches.

Beyond doubt the strongest, most astringent, most scornful and devastating of these words was female. It is clear that Em Pack, the cook, was a female. Females were the tart ones, the dry-lipped ones, the chapel ones, the vinegar-and-starch ones, the horse-facers.

'God A'mighty,' he said, and I thought he gave a shiver. 'There she sat. Like a white toad.'

He gave another shudder and half-amended what he had said by adding:

'Well, not real white. Mucky white. But jist like a toad.'

It is difficult to give any idea of my Uncle Silas's pronunciation of the word toad. On his lips it became a sort of ripe snarl, long and scornful:

'There she wur a-sittin' in a big four-poster, like an old white tooooooard.'

Her mouth, he said, was wide and drooping, the upper lip thick and overhanging the other, like an eave. The flesh of the neck was deeply baggy, hanging like a dewlap, pulsating slowly and sloppily up and down as she breathed. Over the eyes hung thick toad-like lids, creased and drowsy, the eyes themselves bulged and dropsical. Most of the time the mouth hung open, revealing long, yellowish teeth and a pallid, panting tongue.

'Come here. Come closer. What is your name?'

'Voice jist like a toad too,' my Uncle Silas said. 'Croakin' at me.'

'You've been stealing water-cress,' she said.

'On'y a mossel, ma'am,' Silas said. 'That ain't——'

'Are you married?'

'No, ma'am.'

'Come closer to me, come closer.'

He stood by the bed, the clothes of which he swore had not been changed 'since the Christmas afore last, at least,' holding his cap before him in his hands. He was close enough now to see the colour of her eyes. Surprisingly enough they were a sharp deep black and 'I got a funny idea somehow,' my Uncle Silas said, 'that she might have half been a good-lookin' gal at some time.'

'Come closer. Let me look at you. We shall send you to prison for six months, you know that, don't you? The last one went to prison for nine months.'

Again she croaked to him to come closer, and again she accused him about the water-cress. He couldn't understand, he said, why she never mentioned pheasants and he was pondering on this queer omission for the third or fourth time when suddenly she croaked:

'What is that in your cap? Let me see.'

He lifted his cap, remembering the jay's feather he had stuck in it, and before he knew what was happening she had snatched the cap with a cackling croak of triumph from his hands.

'You may go now!' she said. 'You are on bail now. Tomorrow we shall see what we shall do with you. But you are on bail now. Your cap is your bail. What a pretty feather.'

'Now look 'ere, ma'am,' my Uncle Silas said, 'that's damn near a new cap.'

'Is it? Is it? So much the better.'

Cackling again, she put the cap under the bedclothes.

'Now your bail is locked up,' she said. 'Tomorrow morning you must surrender to your bail. Tomorrow morning we shall decide what we shall do with you.'

'Well,' my Uncle Silas said, 'I wur gittin' jist a bit tired o' this 'ere goodly lady an' 'er bail and surrender and I dunno what-all and I said to her:

'Ma,'am,' and here my Uncle Silas took a step closer to the bed, 'I'll give you about ten half-jiffies to give me my cap back or else I'm a-comin' in there to git it. *Wherever* you've got it 'id.'

This threat to her privacy under the bedclothes did not perturb her in the least, my Uncle Silas said.

'Fact on it wur it made her wuss,' he said. 'She shook her fist at me and waggled her ugly old dewlap and said I'd better look out what I wur a-doin' or else she'd have me not on'y for poachin' and trespassin' but for assault and battery too.'

'I know my law!' she said to him. 'I am well up in law!'

'All right, ma'am,' my Uncle Silas said at last. 'I'll be back tomorrer morning. But 'ithout you give me that cap o' mine back mighty sharp I'll git the law on you too. For stealin' other folkses property.'

'Oh! you will, will you?' she said. 'And where are your witnesses? You see, I know my law. You stole four pheasants and a great deal of water-cress and we have witnesses. The last poacher we had here stole only one pheasant and no water-cresses and he got nine months. We know how to deal with poachers.'

She was inclined to talk very fast and by the time she had finished she looked more than ever like a toad with her panting dewlap and her wide mouth slightly slobbering and my Uncle Silas suddenly decided he would give her best for the day.

'You got to 'umour these 'ere females,' he said. 'It's no use you a-forcin' on 'em.'

I asked him now if he got his cap back and what happened and if she cooked him for the poaching but he said:

'Well, I wur back next morning and she wur as sweet as a sugar-ball. You couldn't 'ave 'ad nobody sweeter.'

Here he cocked his eye at me, shook his head slowly and went on:

'That's 'ow wimmin are. Jist like blamed old toads one day, a-croakin' an' a-orse-facin' at you, and the next morning as sweet as summerin' apples, a-dearin' an' a-fussin' on you.'

'You're not going to tell me she deared and fussed you?'

'Oh yis I am,' he said. 'She deared and fussed me for damn near a fortnit.'

I said I was anxious, if he didn't mind, to hear exactly what he meant by dearin' and fussin'.

'Well, it wur funny,' he said. 'Fust it wur "Ad I 'ad me breakfast?" an' then "Wur I tired? Would I like a glass o' beer?" and then it wur "If they was anythink I wanted I'd on'y got to say the word." '

'Crazy,' I said, and it was the only word I could think of for a woman who looked like a white toad, kept a man's cap in her bed and, as in the nursery rhyme, would never let it go.

'Poor gal,' he said.

He shook his head several times, giving once again what I thought was a slight shudder.

'Well, there wur no sense not 'umourin' on 'er,' he said, 'so there I wur, nearly every morning, up there, askin' 'er for me cap and she a-pretendin' she 'adn't made up 'er mind whether to prosecute me or not. Then one day I had a grave to dig up at the church-yard and I never turned up.'

'Trouble?' I said.

'Never sich a gooin'-on in your life,' he said. 'She started 'orse-facin' and a-tunin' and a-bawlin' and I dunno what. "Ma'am," I told 'er, "I wur on'y diggin' a grave and folkses got to be buried, ain't they?" '

'Dig mine! Dig mine! Dig mine!' she said. 'Go away now I beg you and dig mine!'

'It wur summat cruel,' he said. 'It turned your 'eart over. I'd 'ad about enough. I'd stopped a-wonderin' a good while afore why old Emily Pack couldn't stand it no longer and so now I said, "Ma'am, I ain't a-comin' up 'ere no more. Either gimme me cap or put me in clink—I don't care which you do. But I ain't a-traipsin' up 'ere no longer." '

The intensely black haunting eyes looked at him from the toad-like face a long time before answering. Then she said, slowly:

'Come back tonight. I've put it away. But I'll find it by tonight. Come up at seven and I'll give it back to you.'

He had never seen her by night before. He had seen her only white and creased, toad-like and croaking, by the light of day.

And that evening, when he came up to her, only a candle was burning in a single brass stick by the bedside and she was lying down in the bed. She had brushed her white hair until it lay loose on her shoulders. She did not look so toad-like, he said, as she lay there in the light of the candle; nor was her voice so croaking as before.

'Where's me cap, ma'am?' he said. 'I got to git back to fill in this 'ere grave.'

She turned and fixed him with the intensely black haunting eyes.

'It's here in my bed,' she said. 'Come and find it with me.'

'I bin up to some capers in me time,' my Uncle Silas said, 'but I drawed the line at that one. Clink or no clink, I started for the door. Sharpish too.'

He had hardly reached the door before he heard her shrieking. A second later he turned and saw that she had leapt from the bed.

'There she wur,' he said. 'Starve naked, with a double-barrel gun in her hands.'

'I'll shoot you if you don't stay with me,' she said. She

48

put the gun up to her scraggy naked shoulder and aimed it straight at his face. 'I'll shoot—I will—I'll shoot.'

'I knowed I wur damn near cooked then,' he said to me. 'Lucky I'd got another 'at wi' me. Old deer-stalker I use to wear a-winter times. 'All right,' I said, 'you put the gun down and I'll stay a-long o' you for a minute or two.' So she put the gun down and half a jiff later I throwed the deer-stalker at the candle.'

She fired both barrels at him in the darkness. He dived for the door and the last he heard of her, as he half-fell downstairs, was her voice in a croaking, toad-like wail:

'Dig mine!' she was crying. 'Dig mine! It's time to dig mine!'

He paused and I thought, once again, that his gills showed the faintest sign of pallor.

'Not long arter that they took her away, poor gal,' he said. 'She'd bin away afore, but I never knowed.'

'Dead now?'

'Dead now,' he said.

He shook his head, looking far away from me.

'Did you ever get your cap back?' I said.

'No,' he said, 'but she left me a little summat in her will.'

He paused a little longer this time and then, very slowly, put his hand in his waistcoat pocket.

'Come in envelope with a big wax seal on it,' he said. 'I allus carry it with me.'

In his hand lay a pretty bright blue feather.

'Terrible mockin' sort o' bird, I allus think,' he said, 'the jay.'

The Foxes

My Uncle Silas, not unnaturally, and as might have been expected, had little use for the church.

'Can't a-bear popery and 'umbug!' he would say. 'Can't a-bear folks a-maunderin' an' a-moolin' about in church, singing psalms in night-shirts!'

And it followed naturally on this, also, that he had little use for parsons.

'Fool of the family,' he would say, 'like old Rev. Frog-Face we had here in '93.'

Here he would give an imitation of the Rev. Frog-Face, tall, nasal, drooling, hollow-chested and vacuously dithering, riding a strange sort of bicycle and peering through gold Oxonian pince-nez at the simple, robust world of my Uncle Silas and his fellow countrymen.

' "Marning, marning!" Voice like some old yoe a-lambin'. "Marning, Silarse. And how does the world use you and yours this marning, Silarse?" '

My Uncle Silas thought that, on the whole, his long life, bathed though it had been in much beer and cloaked under a good many adventurous petticoats, had been a pretty good one. 'And arter all it's mine,' he would say. 'I done what I liked with it and took the good with the bad. Anythink wrong wi' that?'

I would assure him that I thought there was, all things considered, nothing wrong with that at all.

'Well, Frog-Face did,' he said. 'He wur allus at me to git me to live it different. Wanted to git me to reform.'

The idea of this formidable prospect made me start to laugh, but my Uncle Silas stopped me instantly.

'Ah! you can laugh,' he said, 'but when a man's 'appy what sense is it a-trying to git 'im to start all over again and be miserable? 'Ithout they're miserable, some folks, they don't think they're good.'

I heartily agreed with this and he went on:

'Allus a-poppin' 'is 'ead over the garden fence and wantin' a word wi' me. Voice like some old yoe a-lambin.' "Silarse! I should like a word in your ear, Silarse, if you don't mind." '

My Uncle Silas would then go on to describe what one of these words in his ear was like and how he himself replied.

'Silarse, not to put too fine a point on it, I hear that you were roaring drunk again outside *The Swan with Two Nicks* on Friday.'

'No, sir.'

'And that you were not only drunk but that you and Sam Twizzle and Plum Walker went out of the public house, took the bridle off Milkman Randall's pony and sold it back to him in the bar.'

'No, sir.'

'Silarse, Silarse, be careful what you say. My many informants have another story.'

'Well, they might do. But it ain't mine.'

'Then do you deny you were drunk outside *The Swan with Two Nicks* on Friday?'

'I do. It 'appened to be Sat'day.'

'And I suppose you also deny that you and your friends robbed Milkman Randall of his pony's bridle and sold it back to him in the bar?'

'I do. It wadn't the bridle at all. It wur the whole 'nation harness.'

'Silarse, Silarse!'

'Well, if he wadn't fly enough to look arter 'isself while he wur tryin' to creep round the barmaid's apron that's 'is look-out, ain't it, not mine?'

This might have been enough, as my Uncle Silas pointed out, to put off any ordinary mortal; but parsons, as he remarked, are often persistent, thick-skinned and nosey to a point of driving an ordinary mortal off his head.

'Course we give old Milkman 'is 'arness back next day. Just a bit o' sport, that's all. Sort of thing we used to do when we was all in beer. Got to do *summat* to mek life worth while. Like that day we sent the landlord o' *The Crown an' Anchor* a tallygram ——. Well, that don't matter. Jist a bit o' sport.'

My Uncle Silas then went on to tell me how, at last, he grew very tired of these essays of interference in the normal, worth-while sport of life and how he resented, above all, the notion that there was no good, no purpose and no future in his kind of living.

'No good will come if it, Silarse, I warn you, no good
will come of it.'

'Well, I don't doubt you're right. But all I can say,
parson, is this. If what's a-comin' is 'arf as good as what's
bin then it won't be a-miss. If 'arf the gals——'

'Wine and women! Wine and women! They've been the
downfall of many a better man that you, Silarse, many a
better man than you.'

'Then good luck to 'em, that's all I can say.'

But terrier dogs and parsons, as my Uncle Silas
remarked, have this much in common: once they get their
teeth in there's no shaking them off.

'Well, I got my chance at last,' Silas said. 'One day old
Frog-Face come a-botherin' and a-pesterin' on me to
shoot an old fox what wur a-tekkin' 'is cockerels.'

He paused and I waited for him to go on; but suddenly
he went off down one of his smaller tributaries of recollection.

'Oh! I forgot to say there wur two on 'em. Curate too.
Lived in that there big rectory under them big cedar
trees. Gloomy old place. You could drive a carriage and
four down the stairs. I jistly forgit the curate's name, but
he wur a lean 'un too. They were a damn good skinny
pair. Both on 'em half-cock.'

'Silarse, I should appreciate it as a very great favour if
you'd have a go at this wretched animal. It has eluded
both of us and everybody else assigned to it.'

'Shootin' foxes? I ain't very gone on that.'

'The animal is a poultry maniac. He had six last night,
four last Sunday while I was in church.'

'I ain't very gone on it.'

'Another week and we'll have nothing left, Silarse. I
beg you as a very great favour.'

'I ain't very gone on it. Besides, Sammy Twizzle's got my gun.'

'There will be a quart of beer for you and for Sam too, I can assure you that——'

'It'll very like be all-night job. A quart don't goo far. I generally reckon a barrel for a thing like a fox.'

'Very well, Silarse, very well. If they are your terms.'

This, as my Uncle Silas pointed out, was something hard to refuse; but before finally agreeing on things he felt that he had, as he said, to point out to the Rev. Frog-Face a serious possibility.

'The last fox I see shot was over at Joey Tylers,' he said. 'An' he come back an' 'aunted 'im. Makin' a terrible noise of a night-time. Cruel. Like a lost soul.'

'I doubt very much,' the Rev. Frog-Face said, smiling, 'if foxes have souls.'

'Don't you believe it, parson,' my Uncle Silas said. 'They're nasty-souled animals, foxes. Especially vixens.'

There are, as no doubt you know, many kinds of foxes.

'And it wur jist as I thought,' Silas said, 'it wur a two-legged 'un. We hadn't bin a-sittin' there on the barrel above hour when up come Tunchy Mackness. Carrying a big sack. Well, o' course, we knowed Tunchy well. Knowed 'im years a-new.'

My Uncle Silas then went on to describe a brief interlude in which he, Sammy Twizzle and Tunchy Mackness sat for half an hour under one of the big cedar trees, working out the night's arrangements.

'Well, we wanted to give Tunchy a fair chance,' my Uncle Silas said, 'so we said to him, "Tunchy, it's like this 'ere. You tek another half dozen cockerels and nip a couple for us and then give us another barrel and we won't say a word. But 'ithout you give us the barrel——" '

There was, I thought, a slight flaw in this otherwise profitable arrangement and I said:

'Eight cockerels while the two of you were on guard?'

'Well,' my Uncle Silas said, 'we wur a-goin' to pretend they was two foxes an' one on 'em took the cockerels while we was a-chasin' the t'other. Anyway, that don't matter. Tunchy agreed and about midnight we bunked 'im off 'ome with the cockerels.'

During all this I had detected an unusual change in my Uncle Silas's behaviour and I was about to remind him of it when he said:

'Don't keep chippin' in all the time. I'm a-tryin' to recollect summat.'

I said I was sorry; I had only wanted to put right what I felt was an important omission. But he ignored this completely and said:

'Any road about one o'clock I made a noise like Bedlam

and Sammy let the gun off twice in the paddock at the back. About five minutes later old Frog-Face and the curate come a-scorchin' downstairs and out into the garden in night-caps and night-shirts, a-bawlin':

' "Silarse! Silarse! Did you get the villain, Silarse?" Voice like some old yoe a-lambin' as usual. "Did you get him, Silarse?" '

At this point my Uncle Silas proceeded to address himself to the Rev. Frog-Face in the sternest possible way, wagging an admonishing finger, as if in fact he were present among us.

' "Parson," I says to 'im, "they wur two on 'em. That's why you've bin a-losin' so many. Dog an' a vixen. Sammy shot the dog out in the field, but the vixen got away! And parson," I says, "I don't envy you. I don't envy you!" '

'Why, Silarse, why?'

'They never forgit, vixens. That's why. They never forgit, especially when they lose a mate, and I'll be burned if that there vixen won't come back and 'aunt you.'

Here my Uncle Silas grinned and cocked his eye at me.

'And what d'ye think old Frog-Face said, eh? "Silarse," he said, "I haven't the slightest doubt you'll burn when the time comes, but that the vixen will come back in supernatural form I cannot believe." What d'ye think o' that, eh?'

My Uncle Silas did not pause for an answer and went on:

' "All right, parson," I says to 'im, "you can supernatural till the cows come 'ome, but I wouldn't be in your shoes for *two* barrels o' beer. Nor yit *three*. And as fer dealin' wi' that there vixen when she comes back I wouldn't be here for *four*!" '

Here he paused most impressively, turning to me with an expression of great seriousness, as if perhaps he had even begun to believe in all this himself.

'You know what we done?' he said.

'No.'

'We went *'ome*,' he said, with great solemnity, 'an' started *thinkin'*.'

With patience I waited to hear the outcome of this remarkable pursuit and after some moments he said:

'Upshot on it wur as Sammy got to know a publican over at Thurleigh what had a tame fox in the back-yard. Brought it up from a cub. Could do anything. Et out o' your 'and. Drink 'arf a pint wi' you if you'd a mind to pay for it. Come like a dog when you whistled.'

At this point I was strongly tempted to ask if it could also sing *The Bluebells of Scotland*, but I refrained and he said:

'We 'ad a bit of a job paintin' on it white, but it didn't look a-miss when we'd finished it.'

'I believe you will burn,' I said under my breath, but he didn't hear me and went on:

'An' it wadn't long afore we got 'im up to old Frog-Face's. They was a big lawn in front of the 'ouse, with these 'ere big cedar trees both sides. So Sammy sat one side o' the lawn and me the t'other. I'd got the fox. Then I started a-howlin' and a-wailin' like a good 'un. It were jist nice an' dark at the time.'

Here, for the second time, he paused to draw a picture of the Rev. Frog-Face and his curate scorching into the garden in night-caps and night-shirts.

'That wur the signal,' he said. 'Sammy give a low whistle and I let the fox goo. God A'mighty, we'd got it trained so well I thought it were gooin' to run up their damn night-shirts—it went that close, boy.'

He whacked his hand down on his corduroyed knee several times, his cheeks wagging with laughter.

'Well,' he said, 'we done that fer about six nights. Not reg'lar, o' course. But jist often enough t'aggravate 'em to death.'

'Upshot?' I said.

'Upshot wur,' he said solemnly, 'as I 'ad a visit from Frog-Face. He were in a terrible bad state. Nerves like frog-spawn. All of a-totter an' a-quiver. Curate couldn't come, poor feller. He were bad a-bed and wuss up.'

He licked his lips with great satisfaction and again I was reminded of what seemed to be a change in his habits, but he gave me no time to discuss it and said:

'Begged on me to shoot it. Went down on his knees an' begged on me. Begged on me—they wur damn near tears in his eyes. "Silarse," he said, "Silarse—I beseech you. Rid us of this gharstly visitation." Well, I couldn't very well say no, could I?——'

'Four barrels?' I said.

'No,' he said blandly. 'No. We didn't want to be too 'ard on 'im. We didn't want to be too 'ard. We didn't want to be greedy. We settled fer three barrels—arter all, it took *three nights* to git rid o' the damn ghost—and twothri pipes o' bacca. And that wur cheap at the price.'

He paused again and gave a slight diabolical start of one eye, remembering something.

'Oh! yis, and we got 'arf a sovereign for the brush.'

'For the *what*?'

'Jist shows you what born fools parsons are,' he said. 'On'y 'arf-sharp, that curate. Wuss'n Frog-Face. 'Adn't got twopennorth o' split peas in 'is 'ead.'

'I think I smell burning,' I said, under my breath, but his ears were quick and he said:

'Wad are you a-mutterin' about? What was you a-goin' to say to me jist now?'

Then I remembered the omission, the change in his habits, and what I thought was his odd behaviour throughout the telling of the tale.

'You haven't had a drop of wine all evening,' I said.

He looked up at me with gloom.

'I know, boy,' he said. 'We've tasted the last on it. The parsnip won't be ready fer a fortnit.'

' "Give us the little foxes," ' I said,—'What time does *The Swan with Two Nicks* close?'

He whipped out his watch from his waistcoat with the alacrity of a man about to start a race between two horses.

'You'll jist be in time, boy,' he said. 'You'll jist be in time!'

'Shall I bring a barrel?'

He leapt up, sprightly as a young hound.

'I'll come wi' you, boy,' he said. 'You'll never lift it. There's a knack wi' barrels. You got to know the knack You ain't many know the knack——'

I took his arm.

'Except,' I said, 'the two-legged foxes.'

The Double Thumb

I HAVE so often described my Uncle Silas as a wicked old reprobate of a liar with a bloodshot eye and a strawberry nose who ate too much and drank too much and worked too little that I sometimes wonder if there is not some other feature about him that would, perhaps, bring him more freshly to mind.

Pondering on this, I can think of nothing more striking than his double thumb.

This thumb was his left one and it had something of the appearance of the leg bone of a chicken flattened out at the end. It was very horny, very rough and just about double the size of an ordinary thumb. The nail was double too, with just a suggestion of a heart-shaped appearance about it, and very thick and crusty, like an oyster shell.

When I was a little boy my Uncle Silas used to let me hold this thumb in my hand and I used to marvel at it, with its oyster-shell roughness and its wonderful size, greatly.

'Was it like that,' I asked him once, 'when you were born?'

'When I wur *what*?' he said, rather as if a common circumstance like birth had never happened to him or had happened so long ago that, at the age of ninety, he scorned to remember it. '*Born* with it? That there thumb wur a accident. A terrible *bad* accident. I were nearly *killed*.'

'Killed?' I asked him. 'How?' and I was quite horrified.

'That there thumb,' he said, holding it up and giving a look of solemn beery innocence over the top of it, 'saved me life. If it hadn't of been for that there thumb——'

Breaking off, he shook his head sadly, as if the mere awful memory of it were too much to bear.

'When was that?' I started to ask him, but he cut me short and said:

'You hold hard a minute. Don't be in sich a plaguin' 'urry. You hold hard while I recollect it.'

You had to be very patient while my Uncle Silas recollected things. His way of recollecting things was to cock his bloodshot eye on the distances, take a pinch of snuff or two, blow his nose like a foghorn on a vast red handkerchief and gradually let fall slow, ripe, rich crumbs of detail. As a boy I used sometimes to feel as if he were really making up the stories as he went along: a feeling that, as it now turns out, was a perfectly correct one.

'I wur doin' a bit o' paper 'anging at the time,' he said.

My Uncle Silas had tried such a variety of jobs in his long life, from thatching to grave-digging, that I was not at all surprised about the paper-hanging.

'Up at the mansion,' he said. 'Right up the top of the house. Beautiful view up there. All over the river and the park.'

He was going on to tell me how in those days they had hundreds of deer in the park and thousands of pike as big as hippopotamuses in the river when I thought it time to remind him about the thumb.

'Don't be in sich a plaguin' 'urry,' he said. 'I'm a comin' to that as fast as a nag with a pincushion stuck in its behind.'

It took him in fact all of another hour to come to the business of the thumb, but meanwhile he said:

'Well, there I wur a-doing this paper 'anging, pleasant as you like, no hurry and nobody a-botherin' on me. And she a-bringing me a lump of apple turnover and a jug o' beer whenever she could git away upstairs.'

'She?'

'Under-cook,' he said. 'Nice little gal. Plump as a pigeon. Named Lizzie. Very bright brown eyes. Very bright and round. Just like a pigeon.'

He blew snuff from his nose with the big red handkerchief.

'Oh! married, mind y'. Married to a groom named Walt Thomas. Narrer man though. Terrible narrer.'

'And she brought you apple turnover?'

'Ah,' he said and he started to lick his wettish thick red lips in recollection.

'Very nice apple turnover?'

'Very nice,' he said.

'With cloves in?'

'With cloves in,' he said, 'and a mite o' cheese, and them apples as turn pink when they're done.'

I could not help thinking how very pleasant it must have been to be paper hanging in such delightful circumstances, with a nice plump little pigeon bringing you apple turnover and jugs of beer and such a nice view over the river and the park. But I am, as I was then, an inquisitive person by nature and I said:

'When did she used to bring the apple turnover?'

'Well, it all depended,' he said. 'Sometimes she'd nip up of a morning. And sometimes she'd nip up of a evening.'

'Oh, yes,' I said, 'and what about the thumb?'

' 'Course she wadn't supposed to,' he said and I knew the thumb was still a long way away, 'but she were a very kind-hearted gal. Very kind-hearted. Couldn't bear to see nobody suffer.'

I could not swallow at all the notion of my Uncle Silas suffering, especially in these pleasant circumstances of the apple turnover, the beer, the nice view over the river and the park, and the little pigeon, and as if guessing this he said:

'Well, I mean she couldn't bear to think on me up there all alone. It wur 'nation lonely up there at times. I used to git oncommon sorry for meself.'

He shook his head so sadly that I felt uncommonly sorry for him too.

'It wur a big drop out o' them winders too,' he said. 'Fifty feet. Perhaps 'undred.'

I could not think why he suddenly introduced the height of the windows in this melancholy fashion and I said:

'Is that how you hurt your thumb? Falling out of the window?'

'She come up,' he said, 'one evening in late September. I wur papering a box bedroom at the time and I wur havin' a bit of a up-and-a-downer with the paper.'

I was already thinking of asking him if it had been very nice paper when he said:

'Big baskets of roses all over it. Blue 'uns and red 'uns. It wur very tricky, that paper. You'd got to git the blue 'uns matchin' the blue 'uns and the red 'uns matchin' the red 'uns and what it wanted wur really two pair of 'ands.'

'So she helped you?'

'You're gittin' to be a very fly boy,' he said. 'Very fly.'

He blew his nose on the big red handkerchief again, cocked his eye on the distance with that particular ripe, virtuous leer of his and said:

'Ah! She wur kind-hearted enough to give me hand with the paper.'

'And did you get on much better then?'

'Got on,' he said, 'like house a-fire. One minute she'd be up the steps holding the top o' the paper and I'd be down the steps holding the bottom o' the paper. Course we got tangled in the trellis work a bit——'

'I thought you said big baskets?'

'No,' he said, 'when I come to recollect a bit clearer it wur trellis work. A lot o' very tricky trellis work. Well, by the time we'd got tangled up in this trellis work a time or two and I'd had a sup o' beer and a bite o' turnover and she'd had a sup o' beer and a bite o' turnover an we'd untangled weselves it started to git dark all of a pop——'

He suddenly paused, as he often did at the most interesting part of a story, and looked at me with positive sternness.

'I don't want you goin' clackin' all over the shop if I
tell you this,' he said. 'It were a terrible serious matter.'

'The dark?'

'Ah,' he said, 'the dark.'

I could not think of any possible reason for the dark
being such a terribly serious matter and again he fixed on
me an eye of positive, almost reproving sternness as I
asked him why.

'Because,' he said, 'we wur in it. Me an' 'er.'

'Oh?' I said.

'Yis, me an' 'er. The little pigeon. There we wur—
trapped in the trellis work—in the dark—and *'im* a-bawl-
ing upstairs.'

'Him?'

'The groom. The narrer man I told you about it.
Bawlin' his head off, a-shoutin' "Lizzie! Lizzie!" and
askin' where th' Hanover she'd got to. And there she wur

all of a tremble and me tryin' to calm her down and she a-wonderin' what he'd say when he found her there.'

'You could have told him,' I said, 'that you'd got tangled in the trellis work.'

'And me a-wondering too,' he said. 'And him a-bawlin' and her a-tremblin' and me a-wonderin' and him a-bangin' on all the bedroom doors.'

'Did he bang on the door of the boxroom?'

'Like a damn cannon ball!' he said.

'And what,' I said, 'did you do?'

'Hopped out o' the winder,' he said, 'oncommon quick.'

There crossed my mind, for a sickening second or two, the dreadful impression of my Uncle Silas not only hopping out of the window but falling for fifty, perhaps a hundred feet below.

Then he held up his double thumb.

'Jist got out o' the window and hangin' on like grim death outside when the sash fell down.'

With sickening nausea I looked at the horny, flattened, misshapen thumb, unable to say a word. With ghastliness I saw my Uncle Silas dangling there, trapped and saved by one excruciating piece of flesh.

'Did it,' I said at last, 'hurt very much?'

'Onaccountable,' was all he said, 'onaccountable.'

And then, to my very great surprise, there passed over his face a smile of remarkably enraptured cunning, as if he were remembering with great pleasure something other than his pain.

'But wuth it,' he said. 'Well wuth it, boy.'

As if tasting the remnants of something delicious he passed his tongue across his lips and I could only think

66

that he was recollecting the pleasures of the beer, the apple turnover and the cheese.

'Damnit,' he said with sudden ripe enthusiasm, 'I'd a-gone back and let the winder fall down on me other thumb!'

'And why,' I said, 'didn't you?'

For a moment my Uncle Silas did not answer. Then finally he gave me a long, virtuous, solemn and reproving stare.

'Boy,' he said, 'I think it's about time for you to git home for your supper and me to git back home for a mouthful o' wine. You're a-gittin' too fly by half, boy. You're a-startin' to ask a sight too many questions.'

Aunt Tibby

VERY few people ever got the better of my Uncle Silas, whether it was in the business of eating and drinking, fishing or poaching, women or prize parsnips, and about the only person ever to do so was my Aunt Tibby.

I have never quite understood what the name Tibby stood for, but my aunt, who comes from the opposite branch of the family from my Uncle Silas, that is to say the Rivers branch, and an exceptionally proud, sharp branch it is, was a very remarkable woman. She not only out-did my Uncle Silas; she actually outlived him by a year.

For the better part of forty years my Aunt Tibby kept an extremely comfortable, cosy, spotless little public-house called *The Haymakers* on the borders of Bedfordshire. This pub had something of the appearance of an elongated bee-hive. Its walls of white plaster were most pleasantly roofed with a thick brown nest of thatch that curved up and over five little leaded dormer windows. Downstairs the same number of casement windows, each heavy with trim white lace curtains, looked over a garden crowded in summer with orange marigolds, rambler roses, white madonna lilies and huge scarlet and yellow dahlias that lay among their lush dark leaves like splendid fruit tarts fresh from Aunt Tibby's baking.

For my Aunt Tibby, among a great many virtues, some of which were daunting, not to say formidable, others of which were enchanting, was a remarkable cook. Her raised game pies, prepared for the great shoots of Victorian winter-times, were famous. Her hot Irish stew, always ready for hunting men when they came in half-frozen from scathing mid-winter meets, was so excellent that the receipt for it can be found in a volume of English native dishes under the title of *Mrs. River's Hunting Irish Stew, 1885*.

She was also renowned for several other excellent dishes, notable among them Yorkshire pudding, cheese cakes, eel pie and chicken pudding, but among the most singular of her triumphs was her way with mashed potatoes. No one has ever really been near to gastronomic heaven unless he has tasted my Aunt Tibby's mashed potatoes. Smooth, white and airy as swansdown, served with glorious parsley butter, they remain in my mind with the same exquisite pleasure as the pure high white clouds of a childhood summer's day.

My Aunt Tibby was very justly proud and jealous of *The Haymakers*, with its floors scrubbed as clean and white as bone, its parlour cool in summer and snug as a moleskin in winter, its hunting and shooting patronage, and its impeccable standards of country food and drink and comfort, in which the most discriminating of the aristocracy, yeomanry and squirearchy could find absolute satisfaction. And there could never be, in consequence, as my Uncle Silas discovered, any monkey business at *The Haymakers*.

Looking back, I see that I have described my Aunt Tibby's pub, garden, food and drink without having described my Aunt Tibby herself. In some ways this is rather difficult; in another way, not. For in many ways my Aunt Tibby was, strangely enough, not at all unlike an Uncle Silas in skirts.

I do not at all mean to suggest by this that she was a misshapen old female rapscallion who ate too much, drank too much, told too many lies or was fond of slap and tickle in the bar. She was in every way above reproach in these things. I simply mean that she gave the same impression of many-sidedness, craftiness, wisdom and that deep native cunning that was his charm. I simply wish to convey that she was, like him, a very deep one indeed.

She was a fairly tall woman, angular, long-armed and rather iron-clad about the bust. I cannot remember ever having seen her in anything but black. Her hair was black too and was invariably scraped up into a kind of big oval pincushion on the top of her head. Her dresses always had high lace collars, boned at the side, and the only luxury in the way of ornament that she ever permitted herself was a round silver brooch at her neck.

You might well expect from this that her face would be one of exceptional pallor, high resolve and severity. In fact it was a very deceptive face. It was, in the first place, very red. It flamed with myriads of tiny tangled crimson veins and its mouth was sharp and thin. Its deception lay in the fact that because of its redness you expected it to be jolly and because of the thinness of its mouth you expected it to be severe.

The truth was that it was both severe and jolly. The mouth appeared to be full of the sternest unspoken reprimands. It was only when you looked at the bright clear blue eyes that you saw that they were almost constantly laughing. Then you saw that all the myriad crimson wrinkles of her face seemed to be laughing too. And sometimes, to your great astonishment, she suddenly winked at you.

I must here remove what I feel may be one further mistaken impression about her. She was not abstemious. Like my Uncle Silas she very much liked a tot of this or that. She was very partial to a drop of whisky. Under the iron-clad bust she was ripe and warm. She took a drink with her customers and liked a joke at the bar.

But she was also a disciplinarian and what she would never permit, as my Uncle Silas discovered, was any monkey business. She always insisted, for instance, that her barmaids were well-spoken, clean, good to look at and well behaved.

'I like a girl with pride about her,' she would say. 'I'll have no sluts here. I like my girls to be looked at, but they'll behave themselves or they'll know the reason why."

My Uncle Silas was never a very frequent visitor to *The Haymakers*, and after the end of the eighteen-nineties, in fact, he ceased to be a visitor at all.

Why he ceased to be a visitor was one of those things which, for reasons best known to himself, he did not choose to tell me. My Aunt Tibby told me instead.

'About that time I had a very pretty little maid named Thirza,' she said. 'Rather an unusual name, but then she was an unusual girl. Came from a very nice family, four boys and three girls, all the girls very dark and very nice looking. Thirza was the eldest. Dark glossy hair, dark eyes, very nice little figure and very capable hands.'

The reason for my Aunt Tibby's mention of the hands was because, as she explained, the girl was a very capable cook.

'You get girls that are good behind the bar and nice to the gentlemen and so on,' my Aunt Tibby said to me, 'but cooking they can't abide. But Thirza wasn't only good behind the bar and nice to the gentlemen. She could cook. She wanted to cook. She wanted to learn.'

'A treasure.'

'A treasure,' my Aunt said. 'Worth her weight in gold. Quick as a little linnet. In fact that's what she looked like —quick and bright as a linnet and just about as nice as could be. I wouldn't have lost her for the world.'

Another remarkable thing about the girl, my Aunt Tibby said, was the speed with which she would pick up things, and soon my aunt was teaching her to make the famous raised game pies, the Mrs. River's Hunting Irish Stew, the eel pie, the chicken pudding, the cheese cakes and all the rest.

'And then one day,' she said, 'I think it would be the latter part of the summer of '98, I'll be burned if your Uncle Silas didn't drop in one evening.'

'Trouble?'

'Not immediately,' she said. 'You know Silas. He thinks about women a lot, but he thinks of his belly first. I knew what he was after. He wanted to gorge himself on home-brewed and game pie. I used to keep a fair drop of

home-brewed in those days. It came from the farm up
the hill and it was very powerful.'

'Game pie in the summer?'

She stared at me very severely.

'You'd be surprised,' she said, 'how often pheasants
break their necks on telegraph wires.'

And I could have sworn she winked at me.

'Well, he stayed quite a while that night,' she said,
'gorging himself on cold pie and home-brewed and
generally getting sauced up, but it wasn't until he was
nearly ready to go home that he caught sight of Thirza.
She'd been in the kitchen all afternoon and evening,
getting things ready for a big fishing party we had next
day.'

I asked her how my Uncle Silas had reacted to his first
meeting with this delightful creature.

'Uncommon quiet,' she said. 'Too quiet. I didn't like
it at all.'

She went on to say something about still waters running
deep and it was on the tip of my tongue to make a poorish
pun about still Rivers running deep too when she said:

'He was back next day.'

'More game pie?'

'And he was back the next,' she said. 'And the next.
And the next. The reprobate. The old rascal.'

'You must have been getting very short of pheasants
by this time,' I said, and she gave me one of her sharpest,
severest looks.

'Sometimes,' she said, 'I think you're a chip off the old
block. You've got that same artful, mischievous look in
your eye.'

I accepted this flattering comparison with my Uncle
Silas in silence.

'On the fourth visit,' she said, 'I caught him pinching her.'

'Fourth visit?' I said. 'Not only uncommonly quiet. But uncommonly slow.'

'I caught her sitting on his lap in the cellar,' she said, 'and him sitting on a barrel of home-brewed. Very merry and bright and saying he was going to marry the girl.'

'Marry the girl?' I said and I started to say something about how remarkably well my Uncle Silas must have been enjoying himself when she became very severe again.

'I could see myself losing a very, very good girl,' she said. 'One way or another.'

I did not suggest that if I knew my Uncle Silas I knew which way that would be. I merely asked what sort of shindy she'd kicked up about operations in the cellar and how soon she'd got somebody to throw him out of the pub.

She was most affronted.

'Somebody?' she said. 'I can throw them out myself when the time comes, thank you! There's never been one I couldn't throw out yet.'

And she gave me one of those half-stern, half-winking looks that were part of her formidable, baffling charm.

'No: I didn't throw him out,' she said. 'I invited him back the next Sunday.'

'More game pie?'

' "Silas," I said to him, "if you're going to marry the girl you'd better taste her cooking. You can't marry a girl without tasting her cooking. Your belly knows better than that. Come back on Sunday and Thirza shall cook you a pie." '

My Aunt Tibby went on to tell me how my Uncle

Silas, proud and strutting as a peacock, came back the
following Sunday; how she filled him up with all the
home-brewed he wanted; and how at last, in the evening,
she had him sitting down in the parlour, waiting for his
pie.

'"Made and baked by Thirza," I said to him when I
put it down. "That'll show you whether she can cook or
not."'

It was, it seemed, a very large and handsome pie.

'Pheasant?' I said.

'Well, it was very rich,' she said. 'I'll say that. And so
was Silas's face when he took the top off.'

She regarded me for a moment with that almost prim
sternness of hers, without the flicker of a smile.

'I justly forget,' she said, 'whether it had four toads and
eight frogs in it or four frogs and eight toads. Or whether
it was three live eels and two slow worms or——'

Suddenly she broke off and lowered the lid of her left

75

eye with crafty swiftness, giving a pained sigh that reminded me so much of my Uncle Silas when the tales were tallest and the burden of telling the truth was too much to bear.

'Of course,' she said, 'that was many years before your time.'

The Little Fishes

MY Uncle Silas was very fond of fishing. It was an occupation that helped to keep him from thinking too much about work and also about how terribly hard it was.

If you went through the bottom of my Uncle Silas's garden, past the gooseberry bushes, the rhubarb and the pig-sties, you came to a path that went alongside a wood where primroses grew so richly in spring that they blotted out the floor of oak and hazel leaves. In summer wild strawberries followed the primroses and by July the meadows beyond the wood were frothy with meadow-sweet, red clover and the seed of tall soft grasses. ·

At the end of the second meadow a little river, narrow

in parts and bellying out into black deep pools in others, ran along between willows and alders, occasional clumps of dark high reeds and a few wild crab trees. Some of the pools, in July, would be white with water lilies, and snakes would swim across the light flat leaves in the sun. Moorhens talked to each other behind the reeds and water rats would plop suddenly out of sight under clumps of yellow monkey flower.

Here in this little river, my Uncle Silas used to tell me when I was a boy, 'the damn pike used to be as big as hippopottomassiz.'

' 'Course they ain't so big now,' he would say. 'Nor yit the tench. Nor yit the perch. Nor yit the——'

'Why aren't they so big?'

'Well, I'm a-talkin' about fifty years agoo. Sixty year agoo. Very near seventy years agoo.'

'If they were so big then,' I said, 'all that time ago, they ought to be even bigger now.'

'Not the ones we catched,' he said. 'They ain't there.'

You couldn't, as you see from this, fox my Uncle Silas very easily, but I was at all times a very inquisitive, persistent little boy.

'How big were the tench?' I said.

'Well, I shall allus recollect one as me and Sammy Twizzle caught,' he said. 'Had to lay it in a pig trough to carry it home.'

'And how big were the perch?'

'Well,' he said, rolling his eye in recollection, in that way he had of bringing the wrinkled lid slowly down over it, very like a fish ancient in craftiness himself, 'I don' know as I can jistly recollect the size o' that one me and Arth Sugars nipped out of a September morning one time. But I do know as I cleaned up the back fin and used it for horse comb for about twenty year.'

'Oh! Uncle Silas,' I would say, 'let's go fishing! Let's go and see if they're still as big as hippopotomassiz!'

But it was not always easy, once my Uncle Silas had settled under the trees at the end of the garden on a hot July afternoon, to persuade him that it was worth walking across two meadows just to see if the fish were as big as they used to be. Nevertheless I was, as I say, a very inquisitive, persistent little boy and finally my Uncle Silas would roll over, take the red handkerchief off his face and grunt:

'If you ain't the biggest whittle-breeches I ever knowed I'll goo t'Hanover. Goo an' git the rod and bring a bit o' dough. They'll be no peace until you do, will they?'

'Shall I bring the rod for you too?'

'*Rod?*' he said. 'For *me. Rod?*' He let fall over his eye a tremulous bleary fish-like lid of scorn. 'When me and Sammy Twizzle went a-fishin, all we had to catch 'em with wur we bare hands and a drop o' neck-oil.'

'What's neck-oil?'

'Never you mind,' he said. 'You git the rod and I'll git the neck-oil.'

And presently we would be walking out of the garden, past the wood and across the meadows, I carrying the rod, the dough and perhaps a piece of caraway cake in a paper bag, my Uncle Silas waddling along in his stony-coloured corduroy trousers, carrying the neck-oil.

Sometimes I would be very inquisitive about the neck-oil, which was often pale greenish-yellow, rather the colour of cowslip, or perhaps of parsnips, and sometimes purplish-red, rather the colour of elderberries, or perhaps of blackberries or plums.

On one occasion I noticed that the neck-oil was very light in colour, almost white, or perhaps more accurately like straw-coloured water.

'Is it a new sort of neck-oil you've got?' I said.

'New flavour.'

'What is it made of?'

'Taters.'

'And you've got two bottles today,' I said.

'Must try to git used to the new flavour.'

'And do you think,' I said, 'we shall catch a bigger fish now that you've got a new kind of neck-oil?'

'Shouldn't be a bit surprised, boy,' he said, 'if we don't git one as big as a donkey.'

That afternoon it was very hot and still as we sat under the shade of a big willow, by the side of a pool that seemed to have across it an oiled black skin broken only by minutest winks of sunlight when the leaves of the willow parted softly in gentle turns of air.

'This is the place where me and Sammy tickled that big 'un out,' my Uncle Silas said.

'The one you carried home in a pig trough?'

'That's the one.'

I said how much I too should like to catch one I could take home in a pig trough and my Uncle Silas said:

'Well, you never will if you keep whittlin' and talkin' and ompolodgin' about.' My Uncle Silas was the only man in the world who ever used the word ompolodgin'. It was a very expressive word and when my Uncle Silas accused you of ompolodgin' it was a very serious matter. It meant that you had buttons on your bottom and if you didn't drop it he would damn well ding your ear. 'You gotta sit still and wait and not keep fidgetin' and very like in another half-hour you'll see a big 'un layin' aside o' that log. But not if you keep ompolodgin'! See?'

'Yes, Uncle.'

'That's why I bring the neck-oil,' he said. 'It quiets you down so's you ain't a-whittlin' and a-ompolodgin' all the time.'

'Can I have a drop of neck-oil?'

'When you git thirsty,' my Uncle Silas said, 'there's that there spring in the next medder.'

After this my Uncle Silas took a good steady drink of neck-oil and settled down with his back against the tree. I put a big lump of paste on my hook and dropped it into the pool. The only fish I could see in the pool were shoals of little silver tiddlers that flickered about a huge fallen willow log a yard or two upstream or came to play inquisitively about my little white and scarlet float, making it quiver up and down like the trembling scraps of sunlight across the water.

Sometimes the bread paste got too wet and slipped from the hook and I quietly lifted the rod from the water and put another lump on the hook. I tried almost not to breathe as I did all this and every time I took the rod out of the water I glanced furtively at my Uncle Silas to see if he thought I was ompolodgin'.

Every time I looked at him I could see that he evidently didn't think so. He was always far too busy with the neck-oil.

I suppose we must have sat there for nearly two hours on that hot windless afternoon of July, I not speaking a word and trying not to breathe as I threw my little float across the water, my Uncle Silas never uttering a sound either except for a drowsy grunt or two as he uncorked one bottle of neck-oil or felt to see if the other was safe in his jacket pocket.

All that time there was no sign of a fish as big as a hippopotamus or even of one you could take home in a pig trough and all the time my Uncle Silas kept tasting the flavour of the neck-oil, until at last his head began to fall forward on his chest. Soon all my bread paste was gone and I got so afraid of disturbing my Uncle Silas that I scotched my rod to the fallen log and walked into the next meadow to get myself a drink of water from the spring.

The water was icy cold from the spring and very sweet and good and I wished I had brought myself a bottle too, so that I could fill it and sit back against a tree, as my Uncle Silas did, and pretend that it was neck-oil.

Ten minutes later, when I got back to the pool, my Uncle Silas was fast asleep by the tree trunk, one bottle empty by his side and the other still in his jacket pocket. There was, I thought, a remarkable expression on his face, a wonderful rosy fogginess about his mouth and nose and eyes.

But what I saw in the pool, as I went to pick my rod from the water, was a still more wonderful thing.

During the afternoon the sun had moved some way round and under the branches of the willow, so that now, at the first touch of evening, there were clear bands of pure yellow light across the pool.

In one of these bands of light, by the fallen log, lay a long lean fish, motionless as a bar of steel, just under the water, basking in the evening sun.

When I woke my Uncle Silas he came to himself with a fumbling start, red eyes only half open, and I thought

for a moment that perhaps he would ding my ear for ompolodgin'.

'But it's as big as a hippopotamus,' I said. 'It's as big as the one in the pig trough.'

'Wheer, boy? Wheer?'

When I pointed out the fish, my Uncle Silas could not, at first, see it lying there by the log. But after another nip of neck-oil he started to focus it correctly.

'By Jingo, that's a big 'un,' he said. 'By Jingo, that's a walloper.'

'What sort is it?'

'Pike,' he said. 'Git me a big lump o' paste and I'll dangle it a-top of his nose.'

'The paste has all gone.'

'Then give us a bit o' caraway and we'll tiddle him up wi' that.'

'I've eaten all the caraway,' I said. 'Besides, you said

you and Sammy Twizzle used to catch them with your hands. You said you used to tickle their bellies——'

'Well, that wur——'

'Get him! Get him! Get him!' I said. 'He's as big as a donkey!'

Slowly, and with what I thought was some reluctance, my Uncle Silas heaved himself to his feet. He lifted the bottle from his pocket and took a sip of neck-oil. Then he slapped the cork back with the palm of his hand, wiped his lips with the back of his hand and put the bottle back in his pocket.

'Now you stan' back,' he said, 'and dammit, don't git ompolodgin'!'

I stood back. My Uncle Silas started to creep along the fallen willow-log on his hands and knees. Below him, in the band of sunlight, I could see the long dark lean pike, basking.

For nearly two minutes my Uncle Silas hovered on the end of the log. Then slowly he balanced himself on one hand and dipped his other into the water. Over the pool it was marvellously, breathlessly still and I knew suddenly that this was how it had been in the good great old days, when my Uncle Silas and Sammy Twizzle had caught the mythical mammoth ones, fifty years before.

'God A'mighty!' my Uncle Silas suddenly yelled. 'I'm a-gooin' over!'

My Uncle Silas was indeed gooin' over. Slowly, like a turning spit, the log started heeling, leaving my Uncle Silas half-slipping, half-dancing at its edge, like a man on a greasy pole.

In terror I shut my eyes. When I opened them and looked again my Uncle Silas was just coming up for air, yelling 'God A'mighty, boy, I believe you ompolodged!'

I thought for a moment he was going to be very angry with me. Instead he started to cackle with crafty, devilish, stentorian laughter, his wet lips dribbling, his eyes more fiery than ever under the dripping water, his right hand triumphant as he snatched it up from the stream.

'Jist managed to catch it, boy,' he yelled, and in triumph he held up the bottle of neck-oil.

And somewhere downstream, startled by his shout, a whole host of little tiddlers jumped from the water, dancing in the evening sun.

The Widder

ON a day in early July my Uncle Silas and I harnessed
the little brown and cream pony—the one that could take
lumps of sugar off the top of your head—and put her in
the trap and drove over the borders of Huntingdon-
shire, where a lady named Gadsby had a long rambling
orchard, mostly of apples but also a few old tall pears,
surrounded by decaying stone walls on the top of which
bright yellow stone-crop lay like plates of gold.

'Is she an old lady?' I said, 'Mrs. Gadsby?'

'Well, she ain't old,' my Uncle Silas said, 'and she ain't
young. She's a widder.'

Even though I was very small I knew quite well what
widows were. Most of the widows I knew lived in alms-

houses. They were either very portly and jolly or they were very thin and vinegary, with thousands of little cracks all over their shiny porcelain faces, just like old cups. All of them dressed in black and most of them wore little lace caps exactly like Queen Victoria's, with black squeaky button shoes. Most of them suffered from asthma, rheumatics, arthritis or something equally crippling and a few of them actually walked with a stick and sometimes even two.

'Does Mrs. Gadsby walk with a stick?' I said.

'Well, I ain't seed her wi' one,' my Uncle Silas said.

'Those old ladies in the almshouses walk with sticks,' I said, 'and they're widows.'

'Well, there's widders and widders,' my Uncle Silas said, 'just the same as there's apples and apples. Some are a sight different from others.'

'How do you tell the difference?'

'Well,' my Uncle Silas said after some interval of thought, during which he spat twice over the side of the trap in a long swift streak that went straight over the hedgerow, 'if you wur a-goin' to tell whether a apple wur a sweet 'un or a sour 'un what would you do?'

'Taste it.'

'That's jist what you do wi' widders,' my Uncle Silas said. 'Gittup there!'

As he said this he flicked the reins over the pony's back and we started to roll along at a smart pace between little spinneys of ash and hazel and high dusty hedgerows covered with pink wild roses and dykes smothered with meadowsweet and willow-herb. The day was hot and sunny and in the meadows, over the cow pancakes, there were brown sizzling crowds of flies.

Presently my Uncle Silas spat again and said something about 'gittin' a cravin' for summat to wash the dust down' and I thought this was a good opportunity for me to spit too. I wanted very much to spit like my Uncle Silas, in that fantastic way that went as straight as a white bow-shot for five or six yards, but most of mine landed on the mudguard of the trap and the rest down my shirt.

My Uncle Silas was very angry.

'Now don't you git a-spittin' again like that,' he said, 'else I'll ding your ear. This lady we're a-going to see don't like little boys what spit. See?'

I said I did see and he went on:

'Now jist you mind your manners when we git there. And another thing. When I ask you to make y'self scarce you make y'self scarce. This lady don't like little boys what keep a-peering and a-peeping and a-popping up all over the place when folks are talkin'. See?'

'Yes, Uncle.'

'All right then. See as you do,' he said. 'Dammit, gittup there! We ain't got all day.'

I was so used to seeing my Uncle Silas with a pleasant, beery, winking look on his face that I was quite upset to see him shocked and angry. For the rest of the journey I sat quite silent, sorry I had offended him and determined to behave as well as I could when we got there.

Not long later we came to within sight of the orchard, with its stone walls and yellow stone-crop and the square stone house standing between. It looked a very pleasant house, with beds of white and purple stocks outside and big white trees of orange blossom about the door, and I said:

'It looks a very nice house. What are we going for?'

'We're a-goin' to taste the widder's apples,' my Uncle Silas said.

The Widder

I suppose it must have occurred to me that apples in early July are not quite ready for tasting, but I said nothing, determined to be on my best behaviour, and soon my Uncle Silas was knocking on the door of the house, opening it and calling inside:

'You there, Miss' Gadsby? Anybody at home?'

At first I thought there was nobody at home. There was no answer from the house, even when my Uncle Silas called a second and then a third time.

Then somebody laughed from the direction of the orchard. I turned to look and there, coming up from under the big ancient apple trees, carrying a basket of raspberries in one hand and a basket of fat shining red and white currants in the other, was the widow.

She was not dressed in black, as other widows were. Nor was she wearing a cap like Queen Victoria's, nor squeaky shoes. She was not walking with sticks and her face was not like an old cracked cup, shiny and full of wrinkles.

She was wearing a white blouse with pretty leg-of-mutton sleeves, a dark blue skirt and a belt of black patent leather. Her skin was very creamy and her eyes, which were wide and bright, shone gaily with greenish fires. In her ears were rather big dangling earrings, also black, made of jet, and every time she laughed, which she did a great deal, they trembled, swinging up and down.

But the most wonderful thing about her was not the earrings, the green eyes, the leg-of-mutton sleeves or the gay fruity way she had of laughing. It was her hair, piled up high on top of her head like a bright red-gold crusty loaf all fresh and twisted from the baker's.

She reminded me so much of women I saw at fairs, holding rifles at shooting galleries or spitting on their hands as they pulled at skeins of peppermint rock, that I at once became very shy, remembering my Uncle Silas's anger at my spitting.

'Well, come inside, dear. Come inside. Come and take the load off your feet. And who is this fine big young man?'

'Lizzie's boy.'

'Well, well, how are you, dear? Come inside. Do you like raspberries? Come inside.'

Soon we were inside the house, in a pleasant room full of mahogany tables and easy chairs and white china dogs on the mantelpiece, with my Uncle Silas not only taking the load off his feet but washing the dust down with a glass of greenish-yellow wine.

'Very nice mouthful o' cowslip,' he said several times.

'It should be, dear,' she said. 'It's the five-year-old.'

'I ain't so sure,' my Uncle Silas said, holding the glass up to the light, 'as it ain't a shade better 'n the eldenberry.'

'Oh! no, oh! no,' she said. 'You think so, dear? The elderberry's only the year before last, dear. It's not ready.'

'You can never tell if anythinks ready,' my Uncle Silas said, 'until you taste on it.'

She laughed a great deal at that, in her wonderfully gay, rich fashion, her red hair seeming half to topple off her head like an over-sized loaf and the black earrings dancing, and soon she and my Uncle Silas were tasting the elderberry wine.

It was very difficult, as I could see, to decide whether the elderberry wine was better than the cowslip, or the other way round, and my Uncle Silas tasted several glasses while making up his mind. Rolling the wines

round his tongue, cocking his eyes about the room, his
cheeks growing steadily more and more like the flaring
gills of an ancient turkey cock, he gradually took on a
great air of ripe, saucy charm.

'Another piece of caraway cake, dear?'

While my Uncle Silas and the widow were drinking
wine and eating caraway cake I was eating caraway cake
and raspberries. The caraway cake was very buttery and
very good and my Uncle Silas took another thick fresh
slice of it.

'How do you find the cake, dear?'

'Well,' my Uncle Silas said, 'I'll tell you. In one way
it's proper more-ish. And in another way it ain't.'

'Oh?' she said, and I thought she seemed a little
shocked to think that her caraway cake could be criticized.
'You really mean that, dear? In what way?'

'Well, it goos down quite tidy except for one thing.'

'And what would thàt be, dear?'

'The seeds git stuck in your gullet,' my Uncle Silas said, 'and you gotta keep a-washin' on 'em down.'

Again she laughed in wonderful rolling rich peals and soon she and my Uncle Silas were washing down the caraway seeds with more and more glasses of cowslip, her eyes shining more and more brightly, with amazing greenish fires.

All this time I had been wondering if it wasn't time, at last, to go into the orchard and taste the apples. Perhaps my Uncle Silas read my mind about this, because suddenly he turned a solemn eye towards me and said:

'Boy, you recollect what I told you?'

I recollected; I hadn't forgotten how well I had to behave myself or that, when the time came, I had to make myself scarce.

'Do you like gooseberries, dear?' the widow said to me. 'You'll find beautiful gooseberries at the far end of the orchard.'

'Yes,' I said.

'That's it,' Silas said, 'you gooseberry off for half hour or more. Gooseberry off until you bust.'

I knew that my Uncle Silas was very fond of gooseberries too and I said:

'Shall I bring some back for you?'

'Not jist now,' he said. 'We ain't gooseberry hungry, are we?' and as he looked at the widow I thought he winked at her.

Down at the far end of the orchard I lay in the long seeding summer grasses and ate gooseberries until, as my mother would have said, there were gooseberries coming out of my eyes. Some were pure golden; others were reddish pink, like grapes; but they were all luscious as I squirted the warm sweet seeds on my tongue.

But after a time, as it grew hotter and hotter and the midday air quieter and quieter except for the sound of grasshoppers and the voices of yellow-hammers in the hedgerows beyond the wall, I grew tired even of ripe gooseberries and I started back for the house.

The orchard branched off, half way down it, into a disused stone pit down which the biggest of the apple trees grew and the oldest, tallest pears. Under the grassy banks in the pit the air was very hot and still, the shadows dark and compressed under the old high trees.

As I drew level with this part of the orchard I became aware of something very remarkable going on there.

Laughing and shrieking, my Uncle Silas and the widow were running races under the trees. My Uncle Silas had taken off his coat and collar and was running in his stockinged feet. The only thing the widow had taken off was her belt—unless my Uncle Silas had taken it off for her, because it was he who held it in his hands.

'Gittup there, gal!' he kept saying. 'Gittup there!'

Every time he said this the widow gave her rich fruity peals of laughter and when I last saw her disappearing beyond dense masses of apple boughs at the far end of the stone pit she was only a yard or so ahead of my Uncle Silas and all the big red loaf-like pile of her hair was tumbling down.

'Gittup there, gal!' he was calling. 'Git up, me old beauty!'

It was late afternoon before my Uncle Silas and I drove home again. The air of July was still very hot and now and then my Uncle Silas belched into it a fruitier, riper breath of wine.

I did not know at all what to think of the races in the orchard and at last I said:

'Did you taste the apples?'

'Ah,' he said.

'Were they nice?'

'Ah,' he said.

I thought for a few moments before asking another question and then I said:

'Were they sweet or were they sour?'

'Sweet,' he said.

'All of them?'

'Every jack one on 'em.' he said. 'Onaccountable sweet.'

Somehow I could not think that my Uncle Silas, what with the cowslip wine and the elderberry wine and the caraway cake and the races with the widow in the orchard, had had time to taste every jack one of the apples.

'But did you taste them all?' I said.

With tender rumination my Uncle Silas stared across the dusty hedgerows of wild rose and meadowsweet, lovely in the evening sun, and belched softly with sweetish cowslip breath before he answered.

'No: but the widder told me how sweet they all wur,' he said. 'And a widder with a good orchard ought to know.'

The Eating Match

IT was always wonderful at my Uncle Silas's little house in the summertime, with the pink Maiden's Blush roses blooming by the door and the cream Old Glory roses blooming on the house wall and the nightingales singing in the wood at the end of the garden and the green peas coming into flower. But it was also wonderful in the wintertime, when we could sit by the fire of ash-logs, roasting potatoes in their jackets, with my Uncle Silas hotting up his elderberry wine over the fire in a little copper pot shaped like a dunce's cap.

'Never bin able to make up me mind yit,' he would say, 'whether it tastes better hot or whether it tastes better cold.'

'Then it's about time you did,'' his housekeeper would say. 'You bin tastin' years a-new.'

My Uncle Silas's housekeeper was, I always thought, a very tart old stick of rhubarb. She wouldn't let you drop crumbs on the floor and I had to be very careful as I skinned the hot potatoes. She and my Uncle Silas were like flint and steel clashing against each other, always making sparks. The strange thing was that the more the sparks flew the better he seemed to like it. They always seemed, I thought, to urge him on to bigger and better lies.

So also did the hot elderberry wine.

'You've 'eerd talk,' he said to me one evening as we sat over hot wine and hot potatoes, 'about the time I knocked Porky Sanders into Kingdom Come?'

'You told me that,' I said.

'And you've 'eerd talk,' he said, 'about that race I had with Goffy Windsor?'

'You told me that,' I said.

'But I ain't never told you, have I,'' he said, 'about th' ettin' match I had with Joey Wilks at *The Dog and Duck* one winter? That wur——'

'Eating and drinking!' his housekeeper snapped. 'All you think about is eating and drinking! All you think about is your blessed belly!'

'Well, dammit,' Silas said, 'I wouldn't be much catch 'ithout it, would I?'

She gave a great snort of righteousness at that and my Uncle Silas, winking at me, pushed a poker into the fire and started to turn the roasting potatoes over.

'They'll be about another half-hour yit,' he said. 'Jist time for me to tell y' about me and Joey Wilks and this 'ere ettin' affair.'

He poured himself another glass of warm elderberry wine, leaned back and started to describe what kind of man Joey Wilks, a shoemaker, was.

'Big man. About eighteen stone. Shoemaker. Come from Orlingford,' he said. 'Good craft, Joey was. Could mek a good pair o' shoes. But *a terrible boaster*.'

'Of course *you* never have been,' his housekeeper said.

'If I can do a thing I do it and I say so,' Silas said. 'But if I can't do it I don't do it and I don't boast about it, like Joey did.'

'Well, some 'd believe you,' she said. 'But I doubt if Gabriel will when the time comes.'

'We ain't talkin' about Gabriel,' my Uncle Silas said. 'We're a-talkin' about Joey Wilks. And I'm a-tellin' you Joey was a terrible boaster and what he wur always a-boastin' most about wur ettin'. And when he wadn't a-boastin' about ettin' he wur a-boastin' about drinkin'. He wur jis' like that General over in America I heard about once—he wur allus boastin' fustest with the mostest.'

'Keep on,' she said.

He kept on; and presently he was telling me of how Joey Wilks had boasted, one evening in *The Dog and Duck*, how he'd eaten a leg of pork, half a bushel of potatoes, six pounds of sausages, a dishful of baked onions, a big Yorkshire pudding and about a gallon of apple sauce, washed down with about ten quarts of beer, for his dinner the previous Sunday.

' "Elastic belly, Joey, that's what you got," I told him,' my Uncle Silas said. 'Elastic belly and elastic mind. Allus stretchin' it. I bet all you ever had was a mutton chop and a basin o' cold custard." '

G   97

Joey, my Uncle Silas said, didn't like this much; in fact he very much resented it.

' "If you're a-callin' me a liar, Silas," he said, "you'd better look——" '

' "I ain't callin' you a liar, Joey," ' my Uncle Silas said, ' "All I'm a-sayin' is you didn't do it, and if you did do it nobody never seed you." '

Joey got very flustered and blustered about this and at last my Uncle Silas said:

' "Well, if you're so set on it, Joey, my old sport, I'll tell you what I'll do. I'll challenge you to a ettin' match." '

' "Pah!" Joey said.'

' "Ettin' *and* drinkin'," ' Silas said. ' "Hot food or cold food. Which you like. And plenty o' beer. And a bet on the side if you've a-mind to." '

' "How much?" '

' "I'll give you," my Uncle Silas said, "three to one. In sovereigns." '

Several times as he told me this he renewed his warm elderberry wine and once he gave the potatoes a turn in the hot red ashes.

'Well,' he said, 'when we finally got down to it we decided we'd eat jis the same as Joey said he'd eaten that Sunday. Pork and taters and sausage and baked onions and apple sauce and baked pudden. *And plenty o' beer.*'

'That I *don't* disbelieve,' his housekeeper said.

'The landlady at *The Dog and Duck* cooked the grub,' Silas said, 'and we had the match in the back parlour. Course by the time the word got round there was a lot o' money on it. Big bets. Toffs an' all started layin' a lot o' big wagers.'

'Mostly on you I warrant,' his housekeeper said.

'Well, that wur the funny thing,' Silas said. 'They wur mostly on Joey.'

He took another drink of elderberry wine, smacked his lips and said he wasn't quite sure but he was very near damned if it didn't taste better hot after all.

'Well, that started me thinkin',' he said. 'I started thinkin' that if the money wur on Joey and Joey didn't win then it'd be a fly thing if I had a little bit on it on meself.'

'Trust you,' his housekeeper said and now I too had something to say.

'How did you decide the winner?' I said. 'Was it the one who ate most or the one who stood up longest?'

'Well, as it 'appened,' my Uncle Silas said, 'it wur the one what stood up.'

Refreshed with elderberry wine, he went on to describe

how the food was laid out in the back parlour of *The Dog and Duck*: two big legs of pork and another in the kitchen oven, in reserve, and big dishes of onions and potatoes and apple sauce and pudding, and with it two barrels of beer.

'And me at one end of the table,' he said, 'and Joey at the other. Like David and Goliath.'

'How long did it last?' I said.

'I'm a-comin' to that,' he said, 'in a jiffy. What I wur jist going to tell you about wur the beginning. Joey wur a very big man and he rushed in like some old sow at a trough, ettin' wi' both hands. Very big man. Joey was. Very big man. And no manners.'

He paused for a little more refreshment, wiping his mouth on the back of his hand, a little sadly, I thought, this time.

'Well, very big in the belly,' he said, 'but not,' he went on, tapping his head, 'very big up here.'

He went on then to tell us how he and Joey were eating for about eight hours, or it might even have been nine hours, he couldn't justly remember. Anyway it was a tidy while, he assured us. Then, just as they were well on the way with the third leg of pork and the second barrel of beer, he thought he saw Joey showing signs of filling up a little.

'He was a-gittin' very dropsical about the eyes,' he said. 'Oncommon dropsical. More like a pickled cabbage. So I started askin' for another leg o' pork——'

'Good Heavens,' I said, 'where did you put it all?'

'Well, to tell you the truth,' he said, taking a long slow deep swig of elderberry, 'I wur puttin' most on it in a bag.'

'The truth! The truth!' his housekeeper started saying.

'I wonder the word don't scorch your lips! My lord, I don't want to be you when you meet Gabriel that day!'

'I wur a very thin little chap at the time,' my Uncle Silas went on, quite unconcerned, looking at the fire through the dark red rosiness of his glass, 'and I got this 'ere bag sewn inside the top o' me westkit. Then I had a big serviette round my neck and the bag droppin' down a-tween me legs an' all I had to do——'

'All right for the food,' I said, 'but what about the beer?'

'Oh! the beer never worried me,' he said.

'*That's* a true word *if* ever I heard one,' his housekeeper said.

'Well, it wur all gooin' on very smooth,' Silas said, 'when all of a pop I could see Joey wur done for. He'd been going very purple for about hour but all of a sudden he started to go very yeller. A very funny yeller. Then he went very stiff and white, jist like a cold beastin's custard. He looked jist like a dead 'un.'

The prospect of a dead Joey Wilks seemed to scare people, my Uncle Silas said, and everybody started running about, trying to get Joey outside.

'Terrible thing,' my Uncle Silas said, 'couldn't lift 'im.'

He drank sadly again.

'Must ha' weighed twenty stone or more with all the grub and the beer inside 'im,' he went on. 'Couldn't lift him. Took every man jack in the room to git 'im up and out into the fresh air.'

'And I suppose you,' his housekeeper said, 'sat there as cool as a cucumber and watched them do it?'

'I did,' he said, 'there wur nothing wrong wi' me.'

He leaned forward to poke at the roasting potatoes and

as the poker touched the first of them I could hear the crackle of the crisp burnt jacket.

'Well, I say I sat there,' he said. 'I did until I got a chance to nip the bag down the cellar steps——'

'Gabriel, Gabriel!' his housekeeper said, raising her hands to heaven, 'Gabriel, I hope you're listening!'

'Then I went outside,' Silas said, 'and there wur Joey, laid out cold.'

'Dead?' I said.

'Half-way,' he said.

He paused for a few moments, shaking his head sadly, taking the opportunity to refresh himself again with a slow mouthful of wine.

'Fust time I ever see what they wur a-doin' to poor old Joey that day.'

'What were they doing?' I said.

'Butterin' his belly,' my Uncle Silas said. 'Only way to git the swellin' down. Had to keep butterin' on it for two more days.'

'Gabriel, Gabriel!' his housekeeper said, raising her hands again, 'I hope you're listening? I hope you're taking it down?'

' 'Course you can use lard,' my Uncle Silas said to me, airily, 'but butterin' on it's better.'

Calmly, one by one, he started to take the roasting potatoes from the fire. Innocently, with virtuous care, he filled his glass with warm dark wine. Solemnly he raised the glass to heaven.

'Your very good health,' he said, 'Gabriel, me boy.'

The Singing Pig

My Uncle Silas once had a sow that produced a litter of sixteen three times, seventeen twice and finally one of nineteen. She could also sing very nicely. She could sing *The Bluebells of Scotland* and several other tunes, including one my Uncle Silas himself composed for her.

I know all this because once, when he was staying with my grandfather and grandmother, he told me so.

'Now about this 'ere tune I med up for the sow. It wur about an old gal what——'

'That's right!' my grandmother said. 'Fill the child's head with more nonsense! Make up a few more tales! I'll be burned if he won't end up as bad as you are!'

'Now look 'ere,' my Uncle Silas said, 'it's all very well you a-gittin' obstropolus about it, but I'm a-tellin' on you she *could* sing. And I'm a-tellin' on you she could sing because I *'eard* her sing. And so did George here. Didn't you, George?'

George was my grandfather. He was a very mild, gentle man, not at all given to being obstropolus, as my Uncle Silas said of my grandmother, but most anxious at all costs to keep peace with the world.

'Well, I don't——' he started to say.

'And it's no use you a-wellin' and a-don'tin', George,' my Uncle Silas said, 'because you wur there. You 'eard her as plain as I did. I 'eard her a time or two afore you did, but you wur there that night when——'

'What night?' my grandmother snapped. 'Some night you were well soaked, I warrant. If it were one o' *them* nights I shouldn't wonder what you *did* hear. Old Nick a-whistlin' down your neck very likely.'

'I'm a-talkin',' my Uncle Silas said, with great solemnity and a certain sadness of eye, 'if you'll give me a chance, about the night the old gal died.'

It was always rather touching, I felt, when my Uncle Silas revealed that certain sadness of eye. Suddenly he would draw from his breeches' pocket his big red hand-kerchief, lift it to his face as if to wipe away a dewdrop or a tear and then, solemnly, slowly, sadly, let it fall to his lap.

There was in this gesture a certain element of fatalism, a faint suggestion of the last rites. It was also rather as if my Uncle Silas knew perfectly well that he was asking you to believe in the impossible and was resigning himself to the fact that you were, at the same time, a person of pitiful, puny belief.

'Arter all,' he would say, 'you git dogs what can dance on their hind legs an' count numbers an' do tricks. You git talkin' jackdaws and performing fleas. An' I knowed a chap at Bedford once what had talkin' hens——'

'We had a talking hen once!' I said. 'It used to talk when you took it corn——'

'There y'are, you see,' my Uncle Silas said with bland and wonderful innocence, 'jist what I'm a-tellin' you.'

'I don't know what I'm standing here for, listening to your tomfool tales,' my grandmother said in tart disgust, 'when I've got starching and ironing to do——'

After my grandmother had flounced from the room my Uncle Silas suddenly winked at my grandfather and started whispering.

'George,' he said, 'nip out the front door and underneath the back seat o' the trap you'll see me medicine bottles. Two on 'em. And on your way back bring me a wine glass.'

While my grandfather was out of the house my Uncle Silas blew his nose several times on his red handkerchief and once or twice coughed very heavily. I was quite worried by this and said:

'Have you got croop? Is that what your medicine's for?'

'Well, it ain't exactly croop, boy,' he said, 'an' yit it is. I git a terrible dry ticklin' now and then in me gizzard.'

'Like hens do?'

'Well, I'm an old cockerel,' my Uncle Silas said. 'And it's allus wuss wi' cockerels.'

Presently my grandfather was back with the wine glass and my Uncle Silas's medicine. There were two kinds of medicine, one pale yellow, the other a deep tawny red.

'I hate medicine,' I said.

'Quite right, boy, quite right,' my Uncle Silas said and started pouring himself a glass of the red medicine. 'Terrible stuff, the way it hangs round your gills.'

A moment later the glass of red medicine disappeared with remarkable swiftness and my Uncle Silas was saying, as he smacked his lips loudly, 'Allus git it down quick, boy, like that. Then it don't taste so bad.' At the same time he started pouring himself a glass of the yellow medicine and presently that too disappeared, also with remarkable speed.

From the cunning smile on my Uncle Silas's face and the fruity way he smacked his lips several times I somehow got the impression that the medicine was, perhaps, not quite so bad after all.

'Is it nasty?' I said.

'Well, it *is*,' my Uncle Silas said, 'but I think I must be a-gittin' used to it.'

He then put the two bottles of medicine into his jacket pocket and hid the wine glass behind the back of the chair. Then he settled back in the chair, gave a series of ripe, rumbling belches, wiped his lips with his red handkerchief, and said blandly:

'Boy, I can feel it slippin' down and a-doin' me a bit o' good a'ready.'

For a moment the crusty lids dropped over his eyes and he looked for all the world like a sleepy old cock about to drop off to sleep and I said:

'Don't go to sleep, Uncle. You said you'd tell me about the pig.'

He cocked one eye open.

'Ah, the old gal.'

And for the second time he made that sad and regretful gesture of resignation, dropping his handkerchief on his knee.

'Well, I bought her one day at Nenweald market,' he said. 'She wur about six weeks then and I was drivin' her

steady on back home—course you know about drivin'
pigs don't you?'

'Yes,' I said. 'You mustn't hurry them.'

'That's right,' he said. 'Well, we jogged steady on and
when we got to *The Bull* at Souldrop I could see she
needed a rest. So I tied her up in the yard and went
inside, and I wur jist about gittin' to know what the
inside of a mug looked like when a chap named Charlie
Sanders come in and said "Silas, that pig o' yourn ain't
'arf makin' comical noises." '

My Uncle Silas then went on to tell me how he went
out into the pub yard and found the pig not, as he was
careful to explain, exactly singing, but making a curious
kind of talking noise, as if she were actually trying to tell
him something.

'Funny thing,' he said, 'but she stopped it as soon as we
started on home. And then I twigged as that wur what
she wanted. She wur *tellin'* on me, see? *Talkin'* to me.

It makes me feel proper queer even now when I think on it.'

My Uncle Silas in fact felt so proper queer that he was forced, a moment later, to take another rapid dose of medicine.

'But you said she *did* sing,' I said.

Smacking his lips, my Uncle Silas said gently:

'Yis, yis. I know. But that wur later. Fust she started to have the litters.' My Uncle Silas for once appealed to my grandfather for both information and support. 'How many litters did the old gal have, George?'

'Well,' my grandfather said, 'she had a fourteen and a fifteen and then the two sixteens. And then——'

'Most onaccountable,' my Uncle Silas said. 'Sixteen, then seventeen and then, dall it, I be damned if she didn't have eighteen. Ain't that right, George?'

'That's right,' my grandfather said. 'And then we thought she were goin' to have nineteen——'

'Don't talk about it, George,' my Uncle Silas said, and once again he used that sudden and resigned gesture of sadness, 'it gives me a turn to think o' the poor old gal.'

So much of a turn did it give my Uncle Silas that suddenly, once again, he was forced to take to medicine.

'But when did she sing?' I said. 'All the time?'

'No, no, no,' my Uncle Silas said. 'No, no, no—on'y at *them times*.'

I naturally wondered about them times and I asked him what they were.

'*Them times*,' he said, 'when she wur in pig. When she were a-havin' on 'em. Ain't that right, George?'

'Well——'

'Did she sing real songs?' I said. 'Like *The Bluebells of Scotland*?'

A certain dreaminess came over my Uncle Silas's face as, for a moment or two, he pondered on this.

'Now you come to say,' he said, 'it sounded uncommon like that the time she had sixteen. Then the time she had seventeen it were jist like *The Rosy Tree*.'

Several times during this conversation I thought how strange and queer and unlikely it was that a pig could sing but whenever I did so I remembered how true it was, as my Uncle Silas pointed out, that dogs could dance and jackdaws talk and fleas perform with little carriages, and my doubts were assailed. But what finally put an end to all my doubts was another sad, sudden dropping of the handkerchief as my Uncle Silas said:

'Yis, she on'y done it at *them times*. When I sat up wi' her o' nights. There I'd be a-sittin' all alone in the pig-sty with the lantin, a-waitin', and all of a sudden she'd start. Then I knowed the little 'uns wur a-comin'.'

Inquisitively and sharply I picked on what I thought was a significant phrase in this.

'All alone?'

'I *knowed* you wur goin' t'ask that,' he said. 'I *knowed* that's what you'd ask. And that's what *I* got a-thinking. There I was all alone wi' her and I thought perhaps I wur 'earin' things. But no,' he went on, 'no.'

Once again my Uncle Silas seemed so affected by his remembrance of things that he took another rapid does of medicine.

'But then your grandfather heard it,' he said. 'That night we both sat up with her and we thought she was goin' to have nineteen. Ain't that right, George?'

'Well——'

'Poor old gal,' my Uncle Silas said. 'I shall never forgit it. Poor old gal.'

Picking up the medicine glass, slowing filling it and holding it up to the light, he seemed to stare through it as if seeing far beyond it the dark little pig-sty lit by nothing but the light of the candle lantern, with the sow breathing her gentle song. This too was what I saw as he described how, on a late October night, he and my grandfather waited for the sow to deliver her largest and, as it turned out, her last litter.

'Too much for the old gal,' he said. 'But she wur a good old gal. She went on singing to the end.'

Slowly, with sadness, my Uncle Silas lifted the red handkerchief and let it fall to his knee; and if there had been a tear in his eye I should not have been surprised to see it there.

'Poor old gal,' he said and as he raised to her memory another glass of medicine I felt like crying too.

Perhaps there are no singing pigs; and perhaps it would be silly, in any case, to cry for them if there were. But then there are a great many people, as my Uncle Silas pointed out, who can't sing either, and I can think of quite a few who do not move me half so near to tears as my Uncle Silas's dying sow and her gentle song.

The Fire Eaters

My Uncle Silas at one time knew two gentlemen named Foghorn Freeman and Narrer Quincey and between them, literally and otherwise, they set the town on fire.

Foghorn Freeman was a big man with a voice that seemed to come, booming and hoarse, out of a cave; he wore crisp sandy military moustaches of splendid outcurving design and had lately returned—it was then some time in the early nineties—from service in India, I think the North-West Provinces, where women were two for an anna and life generally not much more expensive and where little things like setting towns on fire were, it seemed, all in the day's work of a soldier of the Queen.

'All Sir Garnet!' Foghorn used to roar. 'Catch 'em with their ambags down!' Quincey was what my Uncle Silas called 'a narrer-gutted man.'

They were the days when men went off into fits of the blues for three weeks on end, fighting the devil in the shape of street lamp posts and then rushing about the town screaming, 'Don't let 'em git me! They're arter me! Don't let 'em git me!' My Uncle Silas and Foghorn and Narrer also rushed about the town, drunk as newts, tying tin-cans to cats' tails, fighting all-comers, wrecking pubs, putting chamber-pots on steeples, roaring hell and damnation and engaging in other harmless pursuits like letting the fire-horses out at midnight.

'Allus ready for a bit o' fun,' my Uncle Silas said when they rolled three lighted tar-barrels into the middle of the mayor's parade on the Sunday of the Fifty-Feasts. 'Loved a bit o' fun. Liked to enjoy we-selves. Wadn't a man who could stop us either.'

It was about this time that the parson died: an oldish, long-winded preacher, not necessarily killed, but then again not helped, by opening the bible-class lecture on a quiet Sunday afternoon and seeing six demented ducks fly out to the tune of 'Art thou weary, art thou languid, art thou sore distressed?'

In his place came a young man, fresh from Oxford I think, earnest and high-minded and rather short-sighted and with, as my Uncle Silas said, the mouth of a proper fly-catcher. My Uncle Silas had not much use for parsons. They roused the Saxon in him, or something else of that primitive, simple, earthy nature, with a parallel hatred of mealy, fly-catching mouths. Surplices and vestments inflamed him like red rags. Chanters and psalm-singers and Bible thumpers, of which the countryside was all too full, turned him into a healthy fire-eater on the devil's side.

' 'Umbuggin' popery!' he used to rage darkly. ' 'Umbuggin' money-mekking game.'

In the course of a few weeks the young new parson began to speak darkly too.

There were, he said from the pulpit, evil forces abroad. The devil's forces and the devil's voices and devil's hands were at work in the town and everywhere the devil stalked unleashed and unafraid. After my Uncle Silas and Foghorn and Narrer had let the fire-horses out again and rung the Bede House bell at midnight and tied a chamber-pot on the weather-cock he preached, with pain and sorrow, of 'the black trident that is pointed at the heart of this little town.'

'We wur the trident he meant,' Silas said, 'me an' old Foghorn and narrer-gutted Quincey.'

All this time the young new parson was to be seen flying open-mouthed across the small town square, under the chestnut trees, in vivid vestments that changed with flashing bewilderment from day to day, and even from morning to afternoon, according to the demands of the high ecclesiastical calendar. Stoles of gold and purple, glimpses of scarlet silk under long white surplices, beads and crosses—Rome, my Uncle Silas considered, had wormed its evil way into town.

'Even had a hat on,' my Uncle Silas said: as if that, above all, were the crown of popishness. 'A black 'un. Looked like a cross between a saucepan and what we tied a-top o' the Bede House weather-cock.'

'Here's the old gal with his ambags on!' Foghorn would shout across the square. 'Treacle trousers!'

Some time after this Silas had the misfortune, as he

came out of *The Griffin*, blood-shot eye gleaming, red lips
wickedly wet and a certain absence of steering noticeable
in his thick bow legs, to run into the flying figure of
purple and gold and scarlet, complete with canonical
chamber-pot, as it flashed across the square.

'Ah! Silas, I have been wanting for some time to
buttonhole you.'

'Well, 'ere's me buttonhole,' Silas said. 'Now you git
hold on it good an' proper while you got the chance.'

'I did not quite mean it like that. It was a sort of figure
of speech—I——'

'Well then,' Silas said, 'you jis stop figurin' and
speechin' and git on wi' your 'umbuggin' fancy-work
while I goo an' 'ave a wet at *The Dragon*.'

'I think it all too obvious you have had a wet already.'

'Jis' washed me mouth out with a drop,' Silas said. 'I
don't deny it.'

He blew with magnificent and snotty indifference into
his large red handkerchief and the young man said:

'You are a menace to the town. You and Freeman and
that Quincey fellow. People are going in terror. They dare
not go out at nights.'

'Dear oh! dear.'

'I will not tolerate it. It has gone beyond all limits.
Never the one of you is ever seen at church, in God's
house, behaving in godly fashion—you take us back to
the days of bear-baiting and cock-throwing and hooli-
ganism of that kind.'

'Dear oh! dear.'

'You never lift a finger to show regret or mitigation.
You glory in it!—that's worst of all.'

'Yessir.' Silas had a way, sometimes, of lowering his
eyes, of drawing half over them a pair of butter-smooth

lids as meek and bland as a child's. 'If that's the way it is I'm very sorry, sir. What would you like us to do?'

'I should not take it at all amiss if you came to church once in a while——'

'Very well then, sir,' Silas said. 'I ain't much of a church-going man. Nor yit ain't Foghorn and Quincey. But if we can git over there once in a while we will.'

'I appreciate that,' the young man said. 'I truly appreciate it. It only remains to be seen——'

'Yessir,' Silas said. 'It jis' remains to be seen.'

The following Sunday there were Foghorn and Quincey and my Uncle Silas sitting in the front pew at church like a row of innocent owls. 'You never sich 'umbuggin' palaver in all y' damn days,' my Uncle Silas said. 'A-burnin' this and a-wavin' that and a-waterin' summat else. I never sich 'umbuggin' gooin' on in me life. Wuss'n Sanger's Circus.'

'Might think we were a lot o' bees,' Quincey said, 'a-being smoked out of hive.'

During the sermon Quincey, Foghorn and Silas sat listening as if they were made of butter and wondering all the time how soon they could escape and, as Silas said, 'nip over to *The Dragon* and git the taint on it outa we mouths.' My Uncle Silas had never dreamed of such popery. The puritan in him was inflamed as if by heresies. 'Thought they wur never gooin' to be done a-sciencing round in night-shirts,' he said, 'and cock-eyed hats and I don' know what. Never see sich bowin' and scrapin' and groanin' and fartin' about in all me days.'

But after the sermon came an announcement that caused my Uncle Silas to put his elbow in Quincey's ribs and made Foghorn begin to draw meditative hands slowly down his moustaches.

'On the occasion of the celebration of the Jubilee of our dear Queen.' There followed a good deal about homage and prayer, services and singing, solemn thanks and the ringing of bells. And then: 'Of course we shall indulge in secular celebration too. There is to be a tea-fight and a torch-light procession and, of course, a bonfire.'

'You ought to ha' seen old Foghorn's eyes light up,' my Uncle Silas said. 'It wur wuth bein' smoked out for.'

After the service the young parson came to shake hands with the converts to righteousness.

'It has done my heart good. I cannot tell you how it has warmed me.'

'Well, we'll try t' warm you a bit more yit,' Silas said. 'We're learnt a lot foday. Ain't we, Foghorn?'

'Too true,' Foghorn said. 'Too true.'

On the night of the Jubilee they lit the bonfire in the middle of the market square about eight o'clock. The square was packed with people and that, as my Uncle Silas said, 'helped us a lot. In a crowd like that you hardly knowed t'other from which. Half on 'em a bit merry too.'

'Course,' he said, 'I ain't saying me an' Foghorn and Quincey hadn't had a drop o' neck-oil—but then, arter all, it wur the Jubilee. The old gal 'd bin on the throne five minutes and it wur the proper time for a bit of a warm up.'

But the most excited man on the square that night was not my Uncle Silas, or Foghorn Freeman, or Quincey. It was the young parson, carried away on waves of excessive and loyal zeal not merely for his gracious Sovereign the Queen but for that roaring tower of spark and flame lighting up the square and all the streets about the square.

'Keep her going, Narrow,' he kept shouting. 'Don't let

her die down, you fellows! Keep the pot boiling. Splendid, Foghorn! That's a magnificent pile of faggots you have there. Pitch in!'

'Well,' my Uncle Silas said, 'we pitched in an' all good and proper. He kept ravin' for us to bring more wood for the fire and we kept a-bringin' on it. I reckon he must have had two wagon loads o' faggots in the rectory garden. Well, arter we'd got rid o' them and a couple old hen-places and a half a pig-sty——'

'Pile on the agony!' the young parson kept shouting. 'Pitch it on, you fellows, pitch it on!'

About eleven o'clock they started bringing out the furniture. 'Just a few old chairs and things. Nothing much. A couple of old couches and a table,' Silas said. 'Me and Quincey kept bringin' it out while Foghorn looked arter the parson's maid in one o' the bed-rooms.'

That, it always seemed to me, was something much more in my Uncle Silas's line; but he, it appears, had something else to do.

Soon he and Quincey were in another bedroom, rigging up the effigy. 'Fust we got a coupla bolsters orf the bed and then we dressed it up, nightshirt and every mite o' 'umbuggin' palaver you could think on. I should think we put half a hundredweight o' bibs an' cassocks an' nightshirts an' fol-di-dols on that thing. In the finish they wadn't another mite o' popery left we could lay hands on.'

In the other bedroom Foghorn was all this time very successful in keeping the maid quiet and the maid, it seemed, did not mind at all.

'And then Quincey dropped it,' Silas said. 'The pot I mean. We had it on the parson's head and Quincey dropped it. Jist as we was gittin' him down the stairs.'

The pot was china; and up in the bedroom the maid, hearing it crash downstairs, started screaming there were thieves about, but Foghorn—who was a good soldier of the Queen, my Uncle Silas said, with experience both at home and abroad—kept her quiet by telling her it was a cat with a milk-jug.

'Any rate, I found another,' Silas said. 'A beauty. With roses on it. And we put it on the parson's head and took him out into the square. We musta looked jis' like one o' them 'umbuggin' fancy church processions.'

In the square there was so much shouting and singing, so much spark and fire, so much excitement and jollity in celebration for England, the Jubilee and the Queen that the guy with its load of vestments was on the fire and in full flame before the young parson, all merriment suddenly extinguished, saw himself burning away in mockery.

'Burned beautiful too,' my Uncle Silas used to say, in the dreamy regretful way he kept for these occasions. 'Burned beautiful. Pot an' all.'

It was, I used to say to my Uncle Silas in due course, a very successful evening for everybody, not counting the parson, but on the whole, perhaps, a little drastic.

His answer to this was quite pained.

'They wur drastic days,' he said, 'dammit, man! if you never liked somebody you 'umbuggin' well said so. You let 'em know. Bless me heart an' life everybody's gittin' too soft be half nowadays.'

But burning furniture, I used to say, burning a man's clothing, the very cloth and emblems of his calling, with a pot on his head. Not that I minded the pot so much; but the going was altogether a little rough, I thought, a little rough and rude.

To answer which my Uncle Silas used to turn on me his one good eye, the other closed and bloodshot, and say with that bland mock innocence, combined with a certain crooked sternness of his mouth, that he always kept for the finish of some taller tale:

'We enjoyed we-selves, didn't we? Dammit, man, what's wrong wi' enjoying we-selves? I enjoyed it. Foghorn enjoyed it. Quincey enjoyed it. The maid enjoyed it —I know she did, onaccountable well an' all, because Foghorn told me so. Everybody enjoyed it——'

'All except the parson.'

'Oh! yis, well, I know,' Silas said. 'But dammit, it wur only a few bushes and old kitchen chairs and rags we burnt. Don't forget it ain't bin so long since they'd a' burnt *him* too. You ain't goin' to deny that now, are you?'

No, I said, I wasn't going to deny that. But still, burning people out of house and home—that was a bit much, I thought, perhaps a bit too much.

'Dammit, man,' he said, 'you're gittin' as bad as all the rest on 'em. I don't know what the 'nation's coming over everybody nowadays. Everybody's stopped enjoyin' theirselves. Everybody's gittin' too 'umbuggin' soft by half.'

He fixed me with a stare of solemn tartness and disapproval from which for the life of me I could not tell whether he were serious or not, until suddenly he dropped a wicked lid.

'It's about time you had a mouthful o' wine,' he said. 'Git the bottle down.'

Also available in Vintage

W. Somerset Maugham

CAKES AND ALE

'They did not behave like lovers, but like familiar friends...her eyes rested on him quietly, as though he were not a man, but a chair or a table.'

Cakes and Ale is the book that roused a storm of controversy when it was first published. It is both a wickedly satirical novel about contemporary literary poseurs and a skilfully crafted study of freedom. It is also the book by which Maugham most wanted to be remembered – and probably still is.

'A formidable talent, a formidable sum of talents...precision, tact, irony, and that beautiful negative thing which in so good a writer becomes positive – total, but *total* absence of pomposity'
Spectator

'One of my favourite writers'
Gabriel García Márquez

VINTAGE

Also available in Vintage

W. Somerset Maugham

OF HUMAN BONDAGE

'*It was not true that he would never see her again. It was not true because it was impossible.*'

Of Human Bondage is the first and most autobiographical of Maugham's masterpieces. It tells the story of Philip Carey, orphan eager for life, love and adventure. After a few months studying in Heidelberg, and a brief spell in Paris as a would-be artist, Philip settles in London to train as a doctor.

And that is where he meets Mildred, the loud but irresistible waitress with whom he plunges into a formative, tortured and masochistic affair which very nearly ruins him.

VINTAGE

Also available in Vintage

Colette

CLAUDINE
IN PARIS

'Everything that Colette touched became human...'
The Times

At the age of seventeen Claudine is in despair having left her
beloved Montigny for a new life in Paris. Comforted by
her devoted maid Melie, her slug-obsessed Papa, and the
trustworthy cat Fancette, Claudine's instinctive curiosity
gradually leads to an awakened interest in the city.

Ruthless, impetuous and chastely sensual Claudine records
her witty observations and adventures amongst the intrigu-
ing characters that surround her, evoking the glamour and
excitement of Parisian life.

Written with striking realism *Claudine in Paris* is an
inspiring portrait of a precocious young girl on the brink of
transformation into a woman for her, and our, time.

'Her sense of comedy is exuberant; her understanding of
character – within her chosen limits – is profound...
From her imagination images rush profusely forth like bees
from a hive, pollen from poplars, smoke from a cigarette,
nudes from the staircase of the Moulin Rouge, platitudes
from statesmen, or paintings from Picasso'
Raymond Mortimer

VINTAGE

Also available in Vintage

Colette

THE LAST OF CHÉRI

'I devoured *Chéri* at a gulp. What a wonderful subject and with what intelligence, mastery and understanding of the least-admitted secrets of the flesh'
André Gide

At the end of *Chéri* the young Chéri left his aging mistress Léa on the eve of his marriage. Having served in the army during the war Chéri returns to Paris haunted by memories of his carefree youth and the bounty of his benevolent mistress. In the post-war 1920's he finds it impossible to settle down to a new life with his efficient and entrepreneurial wife and friends.

As his looks and his reputation begin to deteriorate Chéri's life is thrown into crisis as he attempts to recapture the contentment and companionship of his luxurious youth. As Chéri and Léa confront each other, and the changes a decade has wrought on their lives and their looks, Colette displays the incredible sensitivity and insight for which she is justly famous.

VINTAGE

H. E. Bates

HOW SLEEP THE BRAVE

'He was without equal in England in the kind of story he had made his own, and stood in the direct line of succession of fiction writers of the English countryside that includes George Eliot, Hardy and D. H. Lawrence'

The Times

First published under the pseudonym of Flying Officer X, H. E. Bates's heroic stories of the exploits of British pilots during the Second World War created a sensation when they appeared in 1942, selling over two million copies all over the world. This book is a one-volume edition of these stories, which first appeared under the titles of *The Greatest People in the World* and *How Sleep the Brave*.

While writing them, Bates lived among the, often painfully young, bomber crews and recorded their lives both in combat and on the ground with a poignancy that deeply moved the generation that lived throughout the war. These tales are immensley readable as an account of the R.A.F. in wartime, reflecting Bates's mastery of both of the art of description and of storytelling.

V

VINTAGE